FROM ASHES

J. E. PACE

Cover art by German Creative

ISBN 978-1-957936-00-0

PROLOGUE

SEVEN YEARS EARLIER

She showed up at half past three. That's a.m. in case anyone was wondering. Rang the bell. A shocking sound at that time in the morning, no matter how long I'd been doing this job, no matter how accustomed I was to the middle-of-the night tones, the sirens long and shrill. Still that doorbell startled me. I jerked out of bed, threw on my pants and stumbled into the main room, fuzzy brained. It rang again.

People come to the fire station sometimes, bringing their emergencies to us, instead of calling 911 for us to go to them. A wreck just outside the station, a man with a bloody forehead from the bar a mile away. And every once in a while—though never in the middle of the night—a homeschool group

1

asking for a tour, or a sweet old lady with a cheese-cake or pie, thanking us for the things we do.

But not tonight. Tonight I released the lock, opened the door. Tonight a woman stumbled in, old car seat dangling from a scarred arm. Sweats and torn tank top. Ball cap covering her face. Not that I could have seen her anyway. She looked down the whole time. I couldn't have told you what color her eyes were even if I'd tried. Her cheeks were pocked though. Scars from picking. Lips chapped. Both forearms lined with old needle scars, though I didn't see anything new at first glance.

Baby set on the floor. Six words. "I can't take care of her."

And the woman was gone, though for a moment her scent lingered, old blood and body odor and something sour from the night.

I peered into the ancient car seat that sat on the floor. A little thing squirmed inside. We hadn't had a surrender for a long time—almost ten months.

I lifted the baby out of the seat—she wasn't even buckled in. I moved the blanket down a notch so I could see her face. The baby opened its mouth—her mouth; the woman had called the baby a girl—and squinched her eyes. I bounced her a second, but still the cry came. Solid. Committed. You had to respect a cry like that.

The engineer, Jessie, came in, suspenders dangling down around her waist, and set a cup of coffee down on the counter. "Been a while." That's all she said, peeking over the pink-gray blanket.

A bruise ran up the baby's forehead in a purple line. Jessie and I looked at each other.

"Did you give the mother your spiel, 'You're doing a brave thing for your baby' and yada yada all that?"

"Nah, I didn't have time. She didn't exactly stay for tea."

"They never do," Jessie said.

They never do.

"She probably didn't deserve your comfort speech anyway," Jessie said, taking a swig of her coffee. "Better get the baby to the ER so they can check her out before handing the kid over to Child Protective Services."

"It really is a brave thing to do for the babies," I say.

"It's the *best* thing," Jessie replied. "That's for sure. Don't know if I can get behind the word *brave*."

She called dispatch to have them page out the EMS unit to pick up a surrender. I bundled the baby up tight.

"You've got a knack," Jessie said, then looked away like she realized her mistake.

My wife and I had been trying. Over two years now. Calendars first, timers, then the drugs. Next step, in vitro, but neither of us was sure we were ready for that. In fact, we were pretty sure we weren't.

My bouncing had turned to a soft rock, then a full on swing. The wailing stopped. Face relaxed, eyes open.

Green as the sea.

CHAPTER 1

PRESENT

*T*he clouds roll in, thick and gray. We don't mind. We're not here to swim, not this time. We watch the fury of sky. Blue to gray, hints of green, sometimes even a wisp of white, like an angel's wing being dragged through sludge. Poor angels.

The rain hasn't started yet and I set a blanket on the covered porch of our rental house. Gabby sits beside me, seven years old. All limbs and eyes and questions. The ocean rages in a choppy reflection of the sky, tumbling, swelling, falling. Sucking in its breath, the shore growing long before letting out a roar, then a series of roars, then a thing that is only a roar. A heart, the ocean. Always beating. Sometimes a soft sway, sometimes a hammering thud, never a still line, a fallen chest, an empty voice.

We often come here on the anniversary of Rachel's death. The house feels too tight, too confined. The ocean still reminds me of her, but freer, easier. Even today, maybe especially today.

Gabby and I look through the pictures of my wife, her mother. "Oh look," I say. "There you are."

She squints at the image, all focus. "Tell me again why I was never in Mama's belly."

"That's not the way you came to us." I'm distracted by the photo—Rachel leans against the counter in the kitchen, a line of sun from the window catching her dark, curly hair, turning a patch of it to bronze. Long legs, tight jeans, peasant blouse slipping off one shoulder.

"I was adopted," Gabby says, interrupting my thoughts in the knowing tone of a second grader. She's known forever, for as long as we could tell her, but she still says it like a new thing, a grand revelation.

"Of course. Best choice we ever made."

"And Mama loved me like if I had been in her belly," she says, continuing the story she'd heard a million times.

"Maybe even better than if you had been in her belly," I say, taking up the narrative. "We'd been trying to have a baby for a very long time."

"How long?" she asks, though I know she knows.

"Two years and four months," I answer.

"But no baby came into Mama's belly," she finishes. She turns the page of the scrap book, and I know what's waiting on the next page.

"None that stayed," I say. "But then—" We both pause, holding our breath at the beauty, the luck, the amazing fact of the next part.

"A baby came," she whispers.

The photo. Rachel and I standing in the foyer, shell-shocked, holding that bundle, now in a clean, handmade pink blanket my sister had sent.

"Brought to me by a woman who couldn't keep her, a sad woman."

Gabby nods solemnly.

A fleeting woman, I think to myself. A troubled woman. But a woman I would never not love, because she'd brought me this child. Rachel and I had been thinking of doing in vitro, but Rachel didn't want it, felt afraid of it—the high hopes, the potential disappointment. After so much disappointment already. And so she'd filled out the forms, begun the process to adopt someone. We'd been told it was a long process, set our hopes on a tall shelf, applied to foster. And then one morning I came home after work with a story of a baby. Green eyes, skinny legs, loud wail. A baby who started to haunt my dreams until one night I woke Rachel, telling her, asking her. And she'd cried. We'd called Child Protective Services the next day, a week after I'd first seen the baby. And because of my job and that connection, because Rachel had already started the paperwork, because it was a surrender with no parental strings attached, the baby came to us for fostering just a few days later. I'd barely had time to set up the crib.

"You gave me a big name," Gabby continues.

"A big name for a baby with a big life ahead of her," I say. "Gabrielle."

"And a big mouth," she says mischievously.

"The biggest I've ever known."

She'd cried for weeks, then months, this child, scrunched into a little ball—knees to belly, all day long. It wasn't drugs, they told us—the mother must have tried to stay clean during her pregnancy—just a strong bout of colic, maybe due to prenatal malnutrition. Colic for months. They warned us of delays. She may not be the same as other children, they said. *All that neglect. That woman.* That was Rachel, Rachel rocking the baby deep into the night.

She gave her to us, I'd added. *And that is good enough.* Taking my turn. Rocking, pacing, always moving.

Gabby turns to the picture of her first birthday, cake smeared in pink and green lines along her cheeks. The first night she slept without waking once. Rachel credited the cake, gave her sweets every day after that. Like magic, Gabby started sleeping, then crawling, walking. When the words had started, they'd barely stopped. 'Dada' first. I'd always reminded Rachel. "It's easier to say," she'd replied. Then my smug smile. One of those jokes that keeps going through a marriage, one you expect to have for all the years to come. All the years, not just two more.

Gabby stops on the picture of her sitting on Rachel's lap. Hospital gown. Bald heads, skinny legs, both of them—dark-haired Rachel finally resembling this little child dropped almost onto our doorstep. But not for long. Soon Gabby's pink cheeks, her stream of words, her questions—soon they kept flowing and Rachel's stopped.

Gabby doesn't turn the next page. There's nothing there anyway, but often she still turns it, and sometimes the things Rachel meant to add, the pictures she ran out of time to add, slip and slide into our laps. But today Gabby closes the book.

"I wish I could remember it better," she says.

"Ah, little girl, no one remembers when they were a baby."

"No, I mean, Mama. I wish I could remember."

I run a hand through her white blond hair. It had

finally started to grow after three years of nothing more than a few straggly millimeters, finally started to grow after Rachel's was completely gone. Now it fell like golden silk through my fingers—straight as a pin, soft as a rose. "That's the way it is with memories, baby girl. They're hard to hold."

"Even for you?"

I don't answer. I don't know how.

"Maybe we should go for a walk, Daddy. Look," she says, pointing to a line of sun lasering down through the clouds.

"Maybe," I say, creaking up from the floor, standing and dusting some stray sand from my shorts.

Gabby holds out a hand and I take it, walking toward that line of sun, that piece of day, that sliver of promise—the same way we've walked every day since Rachel slipped away, lost to a disease, lost to a life that had barely opened up. Gabby swings my hand and I bend down, sweeping her up onto my shoulders as she laughs.

CHAPTER 2

SEVEN YEARS EARLIER

y the time EMS arrived to transport us, I knew. Knew it like falling in love. This was the one. Eyes meeting from across the room, and all that. Those eyes—two tiny green earths—staring from her car seat.

I hefted the car seat into the ambulance and one of the medics stuffed some paperwork into my hands. Technically, I was the official guardian until the folks at the ER took over. I scribbled something, asked casually, "Any idea how people adopt the babies, these surrenders?"

"None at all, man."

Of course.

Jessie grabbed my arm, pulled me aside. "You don't want this one, Aiden. Surrendered baby. Mom all pocked and needled and cut. Baby'll have fits, problems, maybe disabilities. Could be severe. Even if you want it, it wouldn't be fair to do that to Rachel."

Didn't all babies have fits and problems? "I'm just curious, Jessie."

"Sure you are. You think I don't see that look in your eyes. But you gotta trust me. This one's gonna have problems. You saw that bruise. Straight line. Something hit her face."

"You think the mother did it?"

"Doubt it, probably some dude. Or maybe something fell on the kid. While she sat there all day long crying in a nasty diaper. Who knows?"

"Better than a fist, right?"

Jessie shrugged. "Maybe, maybe not. She's gonna have problems."

"Everyone's got problems."

"Not this kind of problems."

CHAPTER 3

PRESENT

*W*e stop for lunch on the way home. The sun has finally decided to make an appearance, and we eat outdoors. Two greasy burgers. Gabby peels the American cheese off of hers, licking at her fingers the whole time. Extra pickles. Soft pink nails. I watch her, amazed at her place in my life, amazed at the throb of life in general.

An hour before we get home, not far from a small town where I sometimes volunteer at the fire station, the car starts to shake. I cross lanes. Just in time. My left rear tire peels into shreds of black. Last time anything like this happened, I was a teenager with a junk car and nowhere to go anyway. I pull our suitcases out of the trunk, rifle around, lifting and banging. Finally find a little donut, which doesn't look much better than the shredded wheel I just lost. I search for a jack while Gabby sits in the grass of the shoulder, searching for four-leaf clovers—like an angel, until she gets bored at my moderate levels of mechanical competence and starts to whine. "Daddy, how loooong?" she says, drawing the final word like eternity has already come and gone.

She's found three four-leaf clovers. None of which are granting me much luck. I hit the wrench, still unable to loosen the final bolt.

"Till I get it," I say, all clipped tones and business. "You think we can get home with just a piece of metal and no tire?"

She harrumphs and re-crosses her legs, twirling the clovers in her fingers. I bang the bolt loose, cutting one of my fingers in the process and hissing in pain.

She looks up, waiting for the bad word. I suck it back in. "Gabby, look in the glove compartment and get me a Band-Aid."

She stands up, all purpose now, opens the passenger seat, and digs through the mess of paper napkins, pens, and random dinner mints leftover from restaurants, finally surfacing with the small first aid kit I always keep there. She putters onto the road and I shout for her to move back to the grass, wrestling all the while to get the almost useless donut onto the car. My little girl sinks into herself, clutching at the Band-Aid in her hand. I finally tighten the last bolt back onto the car just as a state trooper drives up.

"You doing alright, sir?" he asks, getting out of his car.

"Yeah," I grumble, not sure where to wipe my hands. "Just a little trouble with the tire, but I think I finally got it."

Gabby pops her head around the bumper just as I recognize the officer. "Oh, hey Pete. How's it going?"

"Aiden?" he asks. "Man, I haven't seen you in ages. Got a new job, I understand."

"Yeah, few years in now. IT. But I still come down to Davis County to volunteer every once in a while. Not far from here. Saw a few of your cops just last month."

"Where you coming from?" he asks, squatting to look dubiously at my "repair" job.

"Just a couple days in Florida."

"Rain?" he asks.

"Almost the whole trip. But Gabby and I didn't mind."

She holds up the Band-Aid that I've forgotten, along with a wad of napkins that I take gratefully and use to wipe my hands.

"Been raining up here too. You still living in

Haydensboro?"

"Yeah," I say, as Gabby opens up my hand and expertly administers the Band-Aid to my scabbing finger wound.

"Not sure you're gonna make it on this little thing," he says, waving at the tiny, saggy-looking wheel. My buddy's got a shop just a mile down the road. Wisp of a town. Head on over there and tell him I sent you. He'll get you in today. Don't want that pretty little lady stuck by the side of the road twice on the same trip."

"No, I really don't," I say as she hops into her booster and buckles up.

"One mile, on the right. He'll give you a fair price."

"Good to see you, Pete," I say, tossing the suit-cases back into the trunk. "Family doing well?"

"Oldest just graduated, headed out to University of Kentucky last month," he responds. "It all goes too fast. And never fast enough." He grins, stepping into his car.

I slip into my seat and buckle up, gazing into the rear view to check on Gabby, who is now humming a song to her wilting clovers. I catch a glimpse of the green-gray clouds coming up from the south. One mile, on the right. I hope Pete is right about the fair price.

CHAPTER 4

The letter came, as letters do, in a plain white envelope, plastic window over the address. Doctor's office. Not again. Bills still trickled in from our two years of infertility treatments. Things we thought we'd taken care of, things they'd messed up and we had to fix. I sighed and slit it with a penknife, expecting numbers, an hour-long phone call, an inconvenience. Instead, a stream of words. Not long, though they felt like forever. Not difficult, though I had to read them three times.

An appointment. No, a follow-up appointment. To discuss Rachel's biopsy results. Biopsy. She hadn't mentioned such a thing, not one word. A mass. A mass requiring discussion, requiring action, requiring an actual letter.

I called her at work. No answer. Tried her cell. Nothing. "Hey Rach," I said to the voicemail. "Got a strange letter today. Call me."

Gabby stirred from her nap and I checked my watch. She'd only been down for thirty minutes. I heard the scratchy scratch as she crawled down from her toddler bed and fiddled with the door. "Daddyyyyyy."

I set the letter down, opened her door. "Hey baby girl, that wasn't nearly a long enough nap." She looked it too, ruffled and grumpy.

"I want my bottle."

"Ah, no bottle today," I said, grabbing a sippy cup and filling it with milk. "You've gotten too big."

She pouted and her mouth twitched in a way that looked like it might turn to a wail. I shoved the sippy cup at her, tipping it into her mouth, like a bottle. She sucked at it. The letter glared at me from the table and I glanced at my phone. No response from Rachel.

Gabby lumbered into her high chair, then sat, like a queen awaiting her afternoon tea.

I clipped on the tray, set the cup down, and dug through the fridge. I closed it, then realized I hadn't taken anything out. Her mouth was twitching again. "What do you want for lunch today, Gabs?" I asked.

"Gapes," she replied, poking at her sippy in a way that made little drops of milk fall onto her tray.

I pulled out a few wrinkly grapes and grabbed a string cheese.

"I might call Auntie Kate to watch you this afternoon," I said, slitting the grapes in pieces so she couldn't choke on them, then peeling open the wrapper for the cheese. I glanced at my phone again. Empty screen. "I need to do a few errands."

She poked a grape piece in the center with her finger, mashing it into the tray before trying to eat it, then whimpered slightly. I peeled off a strip of cheese and shoved it her direction, but she only had eyes for the grapes. "Here's another, baby girl."

She took it, repeating her actions exactly.

"You really needed a longer nap," I grumbled, scooping up my phone and calling my sister. "Hey, Kate. You got the kids this afternoon?"

"Oh, I've got the kids every afternoon," she replied, and I could hear the cacophony in the other room. My sister had not struggled with fertility issues. Fortunately, she ran the house like she was aiming for some type of military medallion.

"Think you have room for one more for an hour or so?"

"Is she fed, napped, and changed?" Kate asked.

I looked at the pile of mashed grapes on her tray, several bits crusting along her cheeks and the fuzz we called hair. "I'll change her right before I come."

"Sounds questionable," she replied. "Where are you headed?"

"Got called into work."

"No you didn't."

How did she always know?

"Cut my finger off; headed to the ER."

"Keeping trying," she said.

"Sordid affair with another woman," I deadpanned.

"Hmmm, unlikely," she replied. "But it does sound like you got in a fight with Rachel or something."

"No," I responded, looking at the letter. "Not exactly."

"Not exactly," she said.

"Just a bad bit of mail."

"More than a phone call's worth of mail?"

"I called, couldn't get through." I replied, trying to make it seem like no big deal.

"I'm going to be here all afternoon, but I should warn you that Patrick's been puking all morning."

I ran my hand through my hair, looking at Gabby's now thoroughly grape-encrusted head. "I'll be gone, probably less than an hour. You think you can keep them apart?"

Kate paused on the other line. "Patrick's fine," she said. "I just wanted to gauge how important this piece of mail was."

"You're a dirty liar," I said. She should have been a detective, that's what she should have been, a detective or a general, maybe a CIA agent.

"You're the one who said you'd been called into work. Just tell me you need help next time."

"Okay," I said, knowing it was still a lie. I hated to ask Kate for help, hated how organized she was with four little kids underfoot when it felt like I could barely handle one, hated how she knew everything all the time. "Just feels like I need help a lot."

"We all need a lot of help, Aiden. You don't need an excuse."

"I'll be there in about fifteen minutes."

"No you won't," she said. "Gabby's probably going to need a bath first."

I looked at my child with grape face, cheese stick mutilated and drying in her fingernails—weren't those things supposed to be a 'neat' snack? She let out the biggest fart known to humankind—too big, in fact, to be just a fart—and my shoulders slumped. She would definitely need a bath.

. . .

*R*achel wasn't at work. She'd left for lunch and then, according to her receptionist, Macie, she'd had an appointment.

I nodded, turning back through the double doors, feeling the letter in my pocket, stiff and creased. I took it out in the sun, stared at the address on the masthead. Not far from here.

My wife came out an hour later, looking rumpled and small. I'd created an entire battle plan, beginning with me hopping out of the truck, confronting her, demanding a reason for the secrecy. Instead, she saw me almost immediately, sitting there like a stalker. I watched her close her eyes, then tip her head back. I'd seen her do it before—tilting tears back into her eyes. She zipped up her jacket and walked toward me. As though I was some kind of magnet and she had to come, but she didn't want to. She stopped at the window, waited for me to roll it down. "Hey, babe," she said.

That's all, I wanted to shout. "You weren't at work." I said. "I called your cell, too."

"I know," she replied. "I just got your voice message." She waved back at the doctor's office. "Guess we should go for a drive." She walked slowly around the truck, opened the door, and let herself in.

"You don't need to go back to work?" I said. "Don't you have more appointments today?"

"Nah," she replied, looking out the window. "I told Macie to cancel them, that I wouldn't be making it back today."

I drove around the block, no words, none at all coming into my head. She just stared out the window, misting it with her breath, with the heat of her face and cheeks.

"So," I began as we wound out of town onto a curvy country road. "This letter?"

"Cancer," she said abruptly. "I have cancer."

"And you were going to tell me...when?"

"I had hoped never," she replied, still not looking at me.

"Seems like not really the right choice," I said.

"Seems that way, doesn't it."

I cracked my neck, trying to relax, took a curve a little fast.

"Slow down," she said.

I didn't, even though I knew I should.

She noted my disobedience and didn't say anything else, though now she looked out of the front window, not the side, and her mouth had fallen into a flat, thin line. "I had hoped it was nothing."

"But it's not nothing?"

"It's not nothing," she replied.

"And?" I said, still angry, but also worried, really worried. And quiet. Why were we both being so quiet, so stupidly silent?

"Slow down," she said again. And this time I did.

"And?" I repeated, my voice just beginning to rise.

"I didn't want it to be something," she said.

"We've established that," I said, my voice a tight clip.

"And when it was, I figured it still really wasn't, not until I got a chemo schedule or something. If they didn't need to do chemo, then it really would be nothing and I could just not tell you."

"But why?" I asked. "Why not tell me?"

"I don't know," she replied. "Because telling you made it feel more true."

"*Do* you need chemo?" I asked, slowing carefully around the curve, looking for a place to stop, to pull over so I could see her face.

"Starts Monday," she said quietly.

The old Qwik Shop rose up to the right and I pulled into the cracked and weedy parking lot.

"Surgery," I asked.

"No," she replied as I slipped into a faded parking spot.

"Well, that sounds pretty good," I said, putting the truck into park and turning to look at my wife.

But seeing her face, I knew it was not good, not even a little. I frowned. "Why is not having surgery bad?"

"Because the cancer is too far spread," she replied. "There's no one thing for them to take out. They're not sure where it started, though it could have had something to do with why we were having so many problems. At any rate, it's spread to my uterus now."

"So you've been hiding this from me for months?" I said, my voice cranking up another notch.

She turned back to the window, the movement stiff, robotic. "It's only been two weeks, Aiden, a couple appointments."

The fire flared, then left. "Two weeks?" I whispered. "Then how has it spread so much?"

She turned back to me, smiled, the saddest face I'd ever seen. "Because it's been there for much longer than that—the cancer. I just didn't notice. I went in for my yearly and they found a few lumps. And then..." She shrugged, looking just like a little girl. "It was already everywhere."

I cried then. It should have been her. It should have been me reaching up to hold her, to tell her it was going to be alright, that we would beat this horrible thing. Isn't that what tall, strong firefighter guys were supposed to do? Comfort their wives who had cancer. Instead I leaned my forehead onto the steering wheel, shoulders shaking, and my sick wife leaned down, over my back and shoulders, cheek to my hair. "It's okay, Aiden," she said. "It's going to be okay."

CHAPTER 5

PRESENT

he town is small. A gas station, dry cleaner, Chinese restaurant, sandwich shop, plus a couple office spaces—a lawyer, a photographer, a 'For Lease' sign in the space between them. And then, at the corner intersection, Joe's Tire and Body. They've got a Walmart, Olive Garden, and a few fast food restaurants the next town over, closer to where the fire station is. I pull into a spot along the street, which tells me I can only park there for two hours, though I've got my suspicions about whether anybody checks or not. It's hard to be bothered when there are only a few cars on the road. Of course, a bored cop might take the time to be bothered. I check the time and open the door for Gabby, who has already unclipped her buckle. Even from her booster seat, her legs dangle, nearly touching the floor. Soon she'll be tall and heavy enough not to need anything at all. I shake the thought off and swing her down over the curb.

Inside, Joe's smells like soap and new rubber, not the worst combination on earth if you ask me. The floor is surprisingly clean, a few waiting chairs to one side near a basket of scruffy-looking magazines. I barely take any of it in because there's a woman at the desk. And it's not like I've never seen a woman before, but this one is especially striking. Maybe it's that everyone else in the shop, both workers and customers, are variations of guys in baseball caps and t-shirts, or maybe the fresh rubber smell is going to my head. Whatever the reason, the way her long red hair is swept into some kind of braid over her bare shoulder makes my tongue feel a little thick when I look at her. I clear my throat.

Her head is down, clipping a group of papers together, shuffling things away to clear the space in front of her, when my unholy throat-clearing breaks the silence.

She looks up, smiles—a line of white teeth in a face of freckled porcelain. "And what can we do for you today, sir?"

I stand for a second too long. "Uh, tire went out a mile or two away. Coming home from vacation with my girl." I gesture to Gabby. "The trooper who

28

stopped to help said we might find a replacement here."

She looks at the rows and rows of tires—from brand new to moderately used. "Yeah," she says, smiling. "I'd say that's a safe bet."

Feathery earrings brush her shoulders, which I notice are also freckled. And the eyes. Green, just like Gabby's. No wonder I've got a thing for them.

"What size do you need?" she asks. "Looking for used or new?"

"Maybe used," I say. "Just lightly, so it'll match up with the other tire pretty well."

She glances around like she's looking for one of the employees, then notes that there's no one waiting behind me. "I'll just hop outside with you and have a quick look at your car to see how used they are."

"Yeah," I mumble, holding Gabby's hand and trailing behind the woman. "Toyota Camry."

"Should be simple enough," she says. A few strands of her hair tumble against her cheeks. She slips out the door to look at my car and we follow. "This one?" she asks, standing near my car. I nod, and she notes the tire tread on the other tires with a slender ruler. I stand back, staring at her arms, long and bare in the early autumn. Gabby, I notice, is staring too. From wrist to shoulder, this woman has a series of bright tattoos, maybe the most colorful I've ever seen. Flowers, butterflies, roses on vines wound in intricate patterns. A large dragonfly takes the entirety of one shoulder, though her other is bare skin. A bunch of tattoos aren't usually my thing, but there's something about these—as though she's got a garden winding up her arms.

We step back inside and I close my eyes, focusing on the fresh rubber smell—comforting and clean.

She wanders along the walls, stopping at a couple of tires. "This is what you'll be needing," she says as a man comes in, wiping his hands on a rag streaked in black.

"Nora taking good care of you?" he asks and I nod, disappointed in the realization that he's probably the one who is supposed to be helping us while Nora—I take note of her name—mans the desk.

"I think she's pretty nearly got us taken care of," I reply, hoping in a weird way that he'll leave.

Gabby tugs at my hand, looking at me with her big eyes. "Do they have a bathroom?"

The woman—Nora—smiles again. I wish she wouldn't stop. "It's right over there, sweetie, through that door."

Gabby nods shyly and doesn't move.

"Do you want me to show you?" Nora asks.

Gabby nods again.

She hands the man her clipboard, points at a few numbers, and then gestures for Gabby to follow her through the door.

The man is a little grisly—ring of gray hair around a glistening bald head.

"She was very helpful," I say. "Your daughter?"

"Nora?" he asks, glancing toward the door where she and Gabby have gone. "Nah. Though I guess I see how she could be." He laughs a big laugh, and points to one of the tires Nora showed us. "This one'll probably be all you need. Where you guys headed?"

"Just about an hour north to Haydensboro."

"Tires always go out at just the wrong times," he says. "Good for business." Then laughs again.

I want to ask him if his receptionist is single, but it feels like a tacky question.

"Find yourself a seat; there's a pot of coffee if you want some. I'll get this onto your car and you two can be on your way."

Gabby swings through the door, Nora behind. I settle into a chair, rifle through the magazines. Gabby hops up beside me.

"Would you like a cup of coffee, sir?" Nora asks.

"Aiden," I reply. "You can call me Aiden. And, no, I'm okay, thanks."

But Gabby has her head tilted to the side, staring at a large jar of candy on a shelf behind Nora's desk.

Nora gets it down, twists off the lid. "What kind do you like?" she asks.

Gabby looks at me for permission. When I nod, she says, "Chocolate or mint."

"Hmmm," Nora says. "Two of my favorites. I'm sure we can find something in here. Ah, how about this—a little of both." She pulls out a couple Andes Mints and Gabby's eyes light up. Her favorite.

Through the window, I watch them raising the car, taking off the ridiculous donut. I wonder how long it will be. I'm not sure I've ever wanted a tire change to take *longer*, but today I wouldn't mind. Although it's a stupid thought. This town's an hour away. This woman could have a boyfriend, or even a husband—not everyone wears a ring.

"Sure you don't want a cup of coffee?" Nora asks again, jolting me from my thoughts about her empty ring finger.

"Oh, no," I say. "I guess I'm more of a chocolate guy—huh, Gabby?"

My daughter rolls her eyes.

Nora laughs and tosses me an Andes Mint from the jar.

"And your name is Nora?" I say a little awkwardly. I look down and open my wrapper.

"Yup," she says.

"Nice name," I say.

Nora has gotten herself a chocolate as well, along with a bottle of water. "You thirsty, miss?" she asks Gabby, who nods.

"Chocolate'll do that to you." Nora smiles and hands Gabby a bottle of water.

"And you, sir?"

I'm disappointed that she hasn't used my name. "Sure."

She's slipped Gabby a third piece of candy, and I turn to watch the mechanics rotate the wheel of my car. The front door tinkles and an older customer walks in, a cane thudding in front of him. "Where's Joe?" he asks gruffly.

"Out putting on a tire, Phil. What do you need?"

"Dang car's still wobbling," he says. "Any time I go over sixty. I need him to fix it."

The man flops into a seat across from me, scowling at no one in particular. Gabby scuttles a little closer to me, climbing on my lap. Her legs touch my shins and I'm struck again by how much she's grown in just the last few months. It won't be long before she doesn't fit on my lap at all.

Nora hands the old man a coffee. "Joe'll be out in a minute."

"Sure he will," the guy says, shifting his grumpy stare toward me. "You from here?" he asks abruptly.

"No," I say, startled. "Tire went out on our way home from the beach."

He humphs at the information. "Didn't think you looked familiar. You ought to carry a spare."

"I had a donut," I say, "which got me here. But didn't know how well it would do for a longer drive."

"Tell Joe to set you up with a decent spare. A man's gotta take care when he's got such sweet little cargo." He nods at Gabby, something close to a smile on his lips.

"True enough," I say. Joe comes out in time to save me from further cross-examination. "Got your car done, sir," he says to me. "One of the guys will be bringing it out in a minute."

He glances at the older man.

"Car's still shaking," the man says.

"That's cause it's a million years old. You've got the money, Phil. Buy something new."

"I don't want nothing new, just want it to stop shaking."

Joe sighs. "Let's have a look then." He leads the older man out to the garage, where the man had apparently already parked his car.

"Sorry about that," Nora whispers. "That's Joe's older brother."

I laugh. "Say no more. That explains everything."

She laughs, then hands me my bill. Pete was right; it's more than fair. I realize as I look at it that I hadn't even asked on price. "Tell Joe 'thanks,'" I say. "And you too. Thanks for all your help."

"No problem," she says, running my credit card then stapling receipts together and handing me my copy.

"Might have to come back here next time I need a tire," I add.

She nods, not seeming to pick up on the hint, if that's what I just dropped. Did I?

Instead, she files away her copy of the receipt, then glances at Gabby, who has placed one of the clovers on the desk. Nora stares, a strange look passing over her face.

"I think she'd like you to have it," I say, worried she won't understand and might reject Gabby's gift.

"It's beautiful," she says, then takes out a final mint. "For the road."

"I liked that lady," Gabby says when we leave. "We should come here again."

I laugh. I'm already a step ahead of her, standing by the car, inspecting my other tires, suddenly very aware of how old they've become. They'll probably each need to be replaced soon.

CHAPTER 6

FIVE YEARS EARLIER

*T*he night I found out about Rachel's cancer, Gabby toddled into our room, blanket trailing. Such a beautiful thing, a child with a blanket. She was still nearly bald—all eyes topped with a fluff of hair—a baby bird of a child. Originally they'd said her lack of hair was a result of prenatal neglect—her mother going hungry or eating poorly or whatever. But as Gabby grew, developing normally, Rachel had looked at her one night and announced, "Or maybe she's just a blond."

Rachel's chemo was scheduled to start the following Monday—an intense schedule alternating chemo and radiation.

"You should be in bed," I said to our daughter.

Gabby didn't answer. Instead, she went up to Rachel, held her mother's face in her hands, looking serious, like she was about to say something profound. "Monkey," Gabby whispered, the intense green eyes staring into Rachel's brown ones.

We both laughed, Rachel and I, a sweet, strange release from the tension of the afternoon.

"Ah, Gabs," Rachel said. "Where did you last have him?"

We trailed through the house, the three of us, looking for Monkey. High chair, under the table, couch cushions removed and replaced, beneath the bed, in each toy cubby, most of them emptied since the toys were strewn on the floor. We finally found him, fallen off the TV, lying forlorn on a patch of hardwood behind the shelf. "There he is," Rachel said, tucking him into Gabby's elbow and lifting her up into her strong, lean arms. She didn't look like a sick woman, my wife. Dark shiny hair, long legs, curves all over, cheeks flushed from crying and talking, eyes brown like chocolate truffles.

She wrapped our child in all her softness and strength and it all seemed like a big mistake, this diagnosis, this letter that still bent in my pocket when I moved. Maybe I could see a little how Rachel thought it would all go away with a few doctor's appointments.

After Gabby was tucked away into bed, curled like a kitten, bottom poking out, one hand under a fat, soft cheek, Rachel stared, a hard line along her own forehead. "We'll have to tell her too," she whispered when I took her hand. "You'll see how hard it is, how awful to know the words, to speak them."

*A*nd it had been hard, the day we'd said it, the day we'd had to tell her that Mommy would be home in bed, that Aunt Kate would be taking her every day when Daddy had to work. It'd been hard to watch Rachel vomit and thin, her skin becoming paper, her fingers bone. Hard the day she brushed her hair and the chunks fell on her shoulders, sitting there like a forlorn fur scarf. The way she'd looked in the mirror, brushing in steady strokes, until only wisps remained and she'd said to me, still staring at her reflection, "Shave it."

I had. Then wrapped myself around her. Tightly that day. Softer as the weeks went on until one night she said, "I'm so sorry, Aiden, but it hurts too much, being hugged." As though she'd been doing me a favor all these weeks, as though the hugs had been to comfort me and not her. Had they?

I'd lain in bed that night listening to her sleep then wake, breathe then cough, settle and start, and settle again back into a painful sleep. Felt all the slivers digging into my heart. The slivers of her dying, right there under my fingertips, fingertips that had made it my life's mission to rescue, to save, not to sit back and let go. But this was different than a burning building, different than the smoke and flame and cries for help. A quiet that multiplied, a body that shrank, a smile that thinned. And so I buried that first little sliver the deepest—that first slice of hurt—that stab at not knowing, of not being told the first minute she knew she had cancer.

This disease, it wasn't a thing about me. It never had been.

Beside me, Rachel jolted awake again, and I helped her shift and adjust.

The next day, they brought in a hospital bed. Rachel and Gabby played with the buttons, moving the bed up and down, turning on the TV, giggling at the novelty of the bed in the living room. As though they were both children and this was all a game at a sleepover.

I watched, wanting to laugh, but knowing that instead, I was going to cry.

CHAPTER 7

PRESENT

I definitely need another tire. Sure, there are several places in Haydensboro that I could use, but since I got the last one from Joe's Tires, I figure it's best to go back. Honestly, with Joe's prices, it's worth the hour drive anyway. Though prices are obviously not my real motivation.

Gabby brings her pocket dolls along. I've promised her another if she behaves, or maybe a miniature pet. "Will the lady be there?" she asks, surprisingly perceptive.

"Don't know," I say. "Maybe." Hopefully.

We get there just as it opens, a few young employees still shuffling from their cars, an older woman with a bundle of keys by the front door. Her hair is done in a tight gray ponytail, sweater over her arm, coffee in one hand. When she unlocks the door,

I pull it open for her. She smiles and strides in. "Can I help you?" she asks, setting her sweater down, along with a large purse bursting with a newspaper.

I look around a little helplessly. "Is Joe here?" I ask, for lack of anything else to say.

"Not just yet," she replies, sipping her latte. "Usually wanders in at about eleven on Saturdays, sometimes sooner."

Another hour. "Okay," I say, taking Gabby's hand and staring at the tires along the walls.

"Needing new tires?" she asks.

"Just one," I say. "We stopped here last week when one blew out, and I figured I might as well get the other side taken care of, too."

"Well, we don't need Joe for that. I'll call one of the boys in and they'll get you fixed up." I notice that she doesn't take me to the tire wall like Nora did, doesn't offer to help me her herself. I want to believe that Nora was being extra helpful because she was looking for an excuse to talk to me, but she probably just knew more than this receptionist does about tires.

"Coffee'll be ready in a few minutes, hon," she says, opening the door to the garage, and shouting cheerfully for one of the guys to come in.

Gabby and I both look to the shelf for the candy jar. It's not there.

One of the younger men walks in, clean shirt, hands still scrubbed before the day's work begins.

"Just a rear tire," I tell him. "Toyota Camry."

"Don't want to do the other one with it?" he asks.

"Just got it last week. Then thought I might as well match them up."

He rolls one from the shelf and into the garage, just as Joe walks through the front door, bell jingling. "Morning, Miss Brenda," he almost sings.

"Ugh, morning people," she grumbles, nursing her coffee, but smiling.

"Morning?" he says. "It's nearly 10:15."

"Which is definitely the morning," she replies, looking to me for confirmation.

I smile, nod.

He glances at Gabby, who's moving the arms of one of her dolls back and forth, back and forth, already getting bored. "You were in last week. Had the tire that blew."

"That's right, sir. Came back this week to match it up."

"Drove all the way down from Haydensboro?"

"You give the best prices."

"You bet I do." He looks to the place where Miss Brenda is sitting, as though he sees right through my excuse.

I cough into my hand.

Gabby has wandered up to the desk and flopped a dark-haired doll down on the newspaper, while she inspects the woman's crossword puzzle. "Do you have any candy?" she asks.

"Gabby," I scold, but the woman just laughs.

"Oh, you must have been here when Miss Nora was here. Always keeps a stash of candy for the kids."

I look at the empty spot where the candy jar was last week.

"Takes it home on her days off though," Brenda says. "Otherwise, the guys come in here and raid it. You can't trust a twenty-year-old man with a jar of candy."

"So it's her day off?" I ask, trying to sound casual.

"Saturday she's usually off," Brenda says, matching my tone, though a half smile flits across her lips. "I was sick last week, so she did me a favor and came in."

"Got it," I say, wondering if I should just dive in and ask more questions.

"This kid's probably going to be needing his front tires done next week," Joe says, winking at Brenda.

"Undoubtedly," she replies. "Better off to come Friday though. Less of a crowd." She winks back at Joe.

I laugh at the two of them. I haven't been called a

kid for a good ten years. "Okay, okay. Best prices and most beautiful receptionists."

I nod to Brenda and she rolls her eyes, still smiling. She digs into her purse and comes up with a stick of gum for Gabby. "Ask your Daddy first."

Gabby turns to me and I nod distractedly. "Since you've found me out anyway, do either of you know if she's single or not, the receptionist, uh, Nora?"

"Oh, she's single," Joe says, a little something in his voice that I can't pinpoint. "But every guy under forty who works here has asked her out and she hasn't taken a single one up on his offer."

"The girl's just being professional," Brenda says. "Can't go getting involved with a guy you work with. Gets complicated." She gives Joe a conspiratorial look over her newspaper and I realize in a little epiphany that the two of them are a couple.

"Says she's still recovering from a bad break-up," Joe adds. "Though she's been working here for over a year and I don't remember anything with any guy."

My stomach sinks a little. "She does *like* guys, doesn't she?"

Joe smiles. "I've never seen anything with any girl either."

"She's been through some things," Brenda says, scolding Joe. "It's okay for her to take some time."

"Sure," Joe says, then looks at me. "Can't hurt to try to ask her out though."

Can't hurt, I think. Though I know that it *can* hurt a little. Me following a line of rejected guys, one of the masses asking her out and being turned down. Still, I find myself agreeing with Joe. "Yeah, we'll just make it one tire today. I'll have to come back for the front ones later."

"Sure, sure," Joe says. "And rotations and all that. I do a little body work too if you end up needing it."

"Now you're just using me for business," I say.

"Better believe it."

I laugh. "And what days, hypothetically, might be best for business?"

"Monday through Friday, the usual."

"Might have to take the day off work then," I say, looking at my phone.

"Up to you," Joe says. "Like I say, she's a tough nut to crack."

Brenda looks up. "Or maybe most guys just don't know how a woman likes to be cracked."

Joe throws up his hands in surrender. "That's my cue to go check on your car."

He scuttles out playfully. Gabby watches Brenda as she writes several letters into one of the cross-words, each line a hard flick with her pencil. "Any

45

idea what a five-letter river in Germany is?" she asks Gabby, who shakes her head solemnly.

"Me either," Brenda says.

Joe pulls my car out front, tires dark and clean.

"Good luck with the crossword," I say. "Maybe I'll see you next week."

"If you're smart," she replies, not looking up, "you'll scrounge up that personal day and not see me at all."

"She's not too tough a nut to crack?" I ask.

"That's for you to find out, hon." Suddenly Brenda's face lights up and she scratches in her final word. Gabby claps for her.

CHAPTER 8

FOUR AND A HALF YEARS EARLIER

*W*e buried Rachel in the fall. Three short months after the bill came, the one I thought was from the fertility doctor.

People came from at least fourteen states. Her brother from Maine, parents from Indianapolis. Most of her old college roommates and her best friends from dental school. Patient after patient, some crying as they passed me, condolences dropping from their beautiful teeth. The people who worked for her, the receptionist, Macie, bawling like a child.

After the funeral, Gabby drew dozens of pictures. All circles and lines and squiggles of dark hair. Mama and Mama and Mama, memorialized again and again. I chose a large one, stick figure, triangle dress, round hand with five stick fingers extended to the hand of the smaller figure, also in a dress, also extending a hand. I put the date on the back, just like Rachel would have. Father of the year, right here. I pressed on my eyes, cried into my palms, then sealed it into a natural wood frame.

My sister walked in as I worked, set down her mammoth of a purse. "I'm moving in."

I lifted my head from my palms. "Oh, Kate," I said. "I couldn't ask you to do that."

"You didn't," she replied. "I've already unpacked my suitcase in the guest bedroom, so now you can't stop me."

Not the most tender words ever spoken, but I smiled anyway. Even at my best, I couldn't have stopped Kate from doing something she felt she should do. Now, I hardly had the energy to stop a butterfly. "What about your kids?" I asked.

"Todd will watch them in the evenings," she said. "And I've arranged for a friend to bring them here after school. They'll be able to help with Gabby while I help you get things arranged."

"What things?" I asked.

She looked at my closet, tumbling with clothes and dust and memories, then picked up the framed picture. "I'm thinking Gabby's room for this one. Maybe right above her dresser. We'll move the baby pictures to the other wall, and I'll get her winter clothes all dug out so we can box up summer."

"You really don't have to, Kate," I said. "It's too much."

"It is, little brother. And that's why I'm here."

She potty-trained Gabby—the epic toddler battle of the last year, abandoned in Rachel's last months, and now put to rest in a matter of days. She cleaned out the closet, donated, rehomed. Pared down the kitchen so that all that remained were the gadgets I understood. Baked and froze neat squares of home-made freezer meals. Scrubbed the toilet, scrubbed the baseboards, scrubbed the memories. Boxed and reframed. Bite-sized pieces now, manageable. "They'll be there for you when you're ready, Aiden," she said.

And on the night before she left, I came home to find her painting Gabby's nails, though as far as I knew she'd never painted a single nail in the entirety of her life.

"A little zen, isn't it?" she asked. "Minus the smell, I guess."

"Yeah, I'm a pro at it now, aren't I, Gabs?"

Gabby shrugged. "Aunt Kate did pink." My sister had mixed the colors accidentally.

Kate mouthed, *Sorry about that.*

I set Gabby on my lap, blew the tiny nails till they

dried. "Don't tell me Katie's better at drying than I am."

Gabby just giggled and I swung her around. A big smile on my face, the picture of joy, father and daughter dancing in the kitchen. But inside I still hurt, inside everything felt narrow and empty. Outside I grinned. "Now it's time for bed. Your auntie's going back to her house in the morning."

Gabby pouted, all the prima donna of a three-year-old.

"Oh, you can come to my house whenever you want," Kate said.

Gabby rested her head on my shoulder, yawned, still the picture of Raphael's cherubic perfection. Which I guess she was, though everything inside of me felt like a giant Picasso. I carried her to her room, laid her down, tucked her in. Gazed. I'd always been a gazer, but with Rachel gone, it had gotten worse. Some nights I stayed in Gabby's bedroom for over twenty minutes just watching her sleep, feeling her aliveness, her presence, letting it calm me. But tonight Kate was packing up, and I needed to thank her.

I found my sister in the guest room, zipping the suitcase, purse beside it, keys on top, everything ready for the morning like she was catching a flight, not driving her own car just twenty minutes away.

"So," she said, plugging in her phone to charge. "How you doing?"

"I never could have done it without you. You've been a lifesaver."

"Not what I asked," she said, sitting on the edge of the bed.

"I'm doing alright," I replied. "Honestly, I guess I'm trying not to think about it still."

"That reminds me. I left a list of therapists' names who take your insurance on the kitchen counter. Maybe check one out."

"Yeah," I said. "I guess that's what people do."

Kate laughed. Neither of us really liked airing our laundry to anyone we haven't known for at least ten years.

"I really couldn't have done it without you," I said.

"You could have. Just would have taken longer and all Rachel's clothes would have gone out of style. Dinner might have been a little boring."

"And Gabby would be wetting the bed as we speak," I add.

"Maybe," Kate conceded, then paused. "What are you planning to do with Gabby while you work?"

"I'll hire a nanny," I grumbled. "I've got a name from one of the guys at work. His kids are older now, so he doesn't need her. It's an older lady, willing to stay overnight."

Kate nodded. "And if there's a fire?"

I looked at her, trying to dig down to her meaning.

"A bad one," she added.

Ah, there it was. "Then you're the one in the will."

"You haven't got a will," she replied. "But I'll call a lawyer in the morning." She made a quick note in her phone. "Though I don't think a will is really the backup plan you want."

I sat on the bed beside her. I'd been avoiding thinking about it—the danger of my job, the daily risks. Every year at least one of us retired because every ten years at least one of us died.

Kate pulled a flier from her pocket, set it on my lap.

I held it close to my face, the cheerful block letters, the neat rows of information, the promises in bold. A tech course. Eight weeks for a yearly salary starting at sixty-five thousand. A solid income in Kentucky. "Nope," I said. "Too good to be true."

"It's not," she said, flicking on a lamp. "These tech guys don't even have to graduate from college, companies need them so bad. A little training and you're in the field. It's growing so fast no one can even keep up with it. Todd's brother just quit his paralegal job to do it and now he makes double."

"Kate," I began.

"You know you'd be good at it. You're always messing with your computer and phone and cleaning and reprogramming and everything."

"That's not what I'm worried about. It would be pretty cool."

"Then give them a call," she said.

"That's not why…"

She set another paper on top of the flier—a little gray newspaper clipping. "It happened last night," she said.

I ran both hands through my hair, reading the words that seemed to blur in and out of focus. "He was my first chief," I said.

"I know."

"Only fifty-one years old."

Kate didn't reply, just sat there with me as I read again about the fire one town over, about the four lives it took—one of them my first chief, my mentor. Crushed under a trailer that collapsed before he could get out with the person he was trying to save. I pushed against my temples, my shoulders beginning to shake. I hadn't talked to him in a couple of years, not since he'd switched to a company the next city over, but I'd heard that he'd just had his first grand-baby—a girl a little younger than Gabby.

"I'm sorry, Aiden," Kate said. "I didn't mean to upset you so much."

"Naw," I mumbled. "I needed to know, would have found out anyway. Better to bawl here than at the station."

She took the clipping, put in the drawer beside the bed, then unfolded the flier, set it in my lap. She'd circled the number to call in red.

"But I love my job," I said, my voice soft, the pamphlet wrinkled and limp on my jeans.

"I know," she replied, touching my shoulder in a rare show of affection. "But you love someone else more."

CHAPTER 9

PRESENT

$\mathcal{M}$y available personal days blink at me from my screen. I've programmed them in pink. The question is, do I really want to use one in order to—likely—spend a morning driving to a distant town only to get turned down by a woman I barely know? Maybe I'd get an Andes Mint for a consolation prize. I click my phone off.

Of course, a little bit of driving isn't *that* much to lose. And with the day off, I can pick Gabby up from school and take her out for ice cream—a much better consolation prize.

I tap one of the pink-coded days on my phone, claiming it as my own. Truth be told, I've barely taken a personal day since Rachel died. I've gone on vacation every year—summer and Christmas with

Gabby, but those personal days just kind of gape open during the school year, empty holes that I don't want to figure out how to fill. Working is easier. And I like my desk job. Kate was right. I'm good at it. I even find a solid satisfaction in helping people and companies work out problems on their computers, add new programs, simplify, clarify, become more efficient. Nothing could ever quite be like helping someone out of a burning building, but I'm surprised how many figurative buildings are burning in small companies that I can help.

It's a good life, a good work. And now my calendar has a big pink stripe through the middle of it.

---

*W*ednesday comes faster than anticipated. I drive Gabby to school. They're just a few weeks into it and everything still looks shiny and clean, including the purple unicorn backpack that bounces against Gabby's narrow shoulders. I wonder for just a moment where those shoulders had come from—the slight build, the blond hair, those eyes that fill her face. Rachel was all curves and dark lines. And I'm tall, broad, hook-nosed—the Greek side, my mother says.

I angle my car out of the school parking lot, pointing it south and taking a deep breath. Just a couple tires, for a good price; and ice cream with Gabby later. That's what today is about.

So it doesn't make sense that I am completely disappointed to see one of the mechanics manning the front desk when I arrive. "Can I help you, sir?" he asks.

"Just looking to get a couple tires replaced. Joe here?"

"He's around somewhere," the kid says. "Anything in particular you're looking for?" He cranes his neck to try to see what I drove up in. I stare at the candy jar behind him. Sure enough, it's gotten a little low and a pile of incriminating wrappers is sitting right in front of the kid.

"One of my rears blew a couple weeks ago. Thought it'd be good to get the rest replaced too."

"New or used?" he asks.

I look around for Joe. "Got anything lightly used, so the price is lower?"

"Price is always low."

"That's what I keep hearing," I say. "Show me what you've got."

The boy—he didn't look more than sixteen, though I assumed he was probably about twenty—gets up and walks to the rack of tires—the same rack Nora showed me. I imagine her there, that beautiful hair, and then everything around me seems silly. The drive, the kid at the desk, my obsession with the candy jar. "Honestly," I say. "Anything will do, if the price is good and you can get it done quickly."

He points at a couple lightly used tires and I nod, just as Joe comes in wiping his hands. "Nora not back yet?" he asks, glancing at me.

"Not yet," the kid says. "And I'm starving. Mario's always takes too long."

"Worth it though," Joe says.

The kid grins. "Long as they don't mess up my meat lover's this time."

I'm trying to follow. So Nora is here today, but she's out for lunch, picking up some food. Fate is not playing on my side.

"What's the boy got you hooked up with?"

I point a little blankly to a couple of tires. I'd missed his spiel about them. Joe nods like the kid has made a good choice. "We'll get 'em on in a bit. Got a couple cars ahead of you, so might be a minute."

I nod and the two of us share a look.

"He's in a hurry," the kid interjects, and I want— just the tiniest bit—to kick him.

"It's okay," I say. "I can't very well bump ahead of other customers. Y'all just do your best."

"Yes, sir," he says. "I'll try to get them on as quickly as possible. You got the desk, Joe?"

"Yeah, I got it," he says, plunking down and frowning at the wrappers, then shoveling them into a small garbage underneath. "In a hurry, are you?" he says after the boy is gone.

"Didn't think she was here today. Seemed a waste of time to dawdle."

Joe laughs. "Well now you've got a problem. Mario's Pizza is slow as molasses and that boy's quicker than a rabbit on meth. What else we gonna have to get done for you today, so you can stay longer?"

"Ah now, I see how you keep those prices low— just piling the services on your innocent customers." I plunk into one of the chairs.

"Innocent," Joe says. "I hope so, 'cause I watch every guy that comes in like a hawk with that girl. She's had a rough go of it, and I'm a little protective of her." He winks. "Not quite as protective as Brenda, mind you, but I do my best."

"Probably gonna be a quick interaction anyway, if she even gets back in time. And then I'll be on my way."

"We'll see," Joe says, leaning back in his chair as I pick up a grimy magazine and the sounds from the garage spill into the lobby. It's a soothing place, in its way—the pops and hisses almost like music, metered and rhythmic. Joe must think so too, because he's asleep in minutes, leaving me to wonder what he meant by saying that Nora had had a tough time of it. She seemed to be doing fine. Job, friends, a small town, that smile.

I tuck my head in the magazine, trying to shake off the thought. I've only gotten through half an article when that dang kid comes through the door. "Got your vehicle done, sir. Quick as I could."

From the desk, I'm pretty sure I hear Joe snigger. That or he's begun to snore in the chair.

"Thank you," I say, taking my keys. "Got them rotated and everything?"

"All done. Good as new."

I smile weakly, and head to the desk to pay. Joe has roused himself and is trying to figure out the card reader. "Sure you don't need anything else today?" he asks. "We got plenty of other services."

"Maybe another time," I say as a little bell jangles outside. I can't quite place the sound until I see a few of the guys gathered around a blue beach cruiser bicycle. A bike bell. Just like Gabby's. Nora is standing beside the beach cruiser, face flushed, red hair wisping across her face and shoulders, handing out small pizza boxes to different guys. I watch, a bit entranced, or maybe confused. I don't know why it seems so surprising to see her there like that, riding a bike like a young girl. Basket at the front and all. She hands over the final pizza to the kid who did my wheels and I make eye contact with Joe. He nods, but all of a sudden I have no idea what to do. I take my keys, head out to my car. But then it seems like the only logical thing is to unlock my car and get in. I press the button, hear the lock click open. But I've driven all this way, all this stupid way. It's like I'm a kid chickening out when I want to ask a girl to the prom.

Lifting a hand, I wave. She catches my eye, smiles, and tries to wave back, but she's holding her own pizza box along with a bag of something and a large drink. I put my keys back into my pocket. "Can I help you carry that stuff in?"

"Nah, I got it," she says, holding the food and trying to rack her bike. I go to the door, hold it open for her. "Sure you've got it?"

In answer, she balances the box on her head, and somehow manages to lock up her bike.

"You sure do got it," I say. "I guess if the tire store doesn't work out, you could put those skills to work elsewhere."

She lifts the box off her head and says, "Yeah, guess I could always wait tables, huh?"

It made my comment seem trite, like an insult,

which wasn't what I'd meant at all. Desperate, I spit out the first thing that pops into my head. "I was thinking more like the circus. You've got some mad skills."

"Mad is right," she says, making her way through the door. "Maybe next time I'll juggle." She sets the food down on her desk. "No Gabby today?"

For a moment I'm dumbstruck. She remembered Gabby, her name even. And by extension she remembered me.

"Nope, school. We've got a date afterwards though. Gabby and I, I mean."

"Aww, that's sweet," Nora says. "She's a lucky girl. Got the last couple tires done, did you?" She nods outside at my car.

I gaze at the dragonfly tattoo on her slender shoulder, vines winding up and around it. "Seemed like the smart thing to do."

"It was."

Joe stands up, looks at me expectantly.

"Might have to come back another day though. Joe here said I could use a new..." I stall out, gazing at Joe.

"...rear fender," he finishes for me. "Next time you can grab a day off."

"Yeah," I say.

"Well, I'll see you then," she says with that

glowing white smile, several of the freckles wrinkling together on her nose. She reaches a hand into her candy jar and pulls out two peppermints. "One for you and one for Gabby." She narrows her eyes at the nearly-empty jar. "Those boys."

Joe gives me a look that says, *Say something. Ask something.* But for some reason, I'm all talked out. I pop the mint in my mouth and Nora and I smile at each other, like a couple of kids at the lunch table. "Enjoy your pizza," I say.

"Best in town," she replies.

Then I scoot my way out, the door jangling behind me. I didn't quite get my date to the prom, but as I make my way to the car, the sweet mint melting on my tongue, I can't help but feel like it's been a pretty good day after all.

And it's only just begun. I still have an ice cream date with the absolute most beautiful girl in the world.

CHAPTER 10

FOUR YEARS EARLIER

*S*ixty-five thousand dollars, starting salary. As promised. Several recruiters by the end of the IT course. A simple nine to five, half hour for lunch. Typical stuff. I was sure I'd hate it.

When I hung up my heavy red firefighter coat for the last time, Jessie gave me a hug, which she'd never done in the last four years we'd worked together. I sniffed the air. "Do I smell smoke?"

"Probably just got the scent stuck in your nose from that last call. You know how it goes."

"Kids and matches." I pushed open the door to the kitchen.

And then the clapping, stomping, whooping. I couldn't put it together at first. The cake—a bright red engine, covered (ironically) with as many candles as would fit. That was the smoke. "We're gonna miss you," Jessie said as several guys whacked me on the back and a few pulled me in for a bear hug.

I stood, taking in slow measured breaths, trying to keep from bursting into crazy tears. This group, these crews—they'd been my life for so long. A few of them I'd even trained with when we were rookies, most of them I'd worked with for the better part of ten years. They'd all shown up for Rachel's funeral— uniforms on if they'd just gotten off work, the rest wearing suits and buttoned up tight—some of them dripping tears like faulty hoses. Even before that, as the years had rolled on, we'd seen people die, helped people live, gone into crumbling houses and brought people out coughing, or dragged them out with no breath left at all. We'd attended at least one funeral for one of our own, killed by a roof no one had expected to collapse, and several others for fallen firefighters who worked neighboring counties where we helped out when they needed an extra truck. We'd done simpler things too—lifted heavy old people back into bed, helped the medics and the cops on busy calls, cut people out of cars or hunted for bodies flung from the vehicles. We'd argued; we'd laughed. We'd roared down the street together, watched TV on slow days, gone to weddings and— for me—a funeral. How could I leave them?

Someone passed me a piece of cake, which I took

numbly, talking and laughing though later I wouldn't remember a single word. A strange blackout as the memories pressed over the present chatter. Marriages, divorces, kids, graduations, and me—a wife I no longer had, and a new baby girl passed to my arms by a hopeless addict who'd somehow brought hope. I tried to remember the mother, what she looked like, and all I saw were arms lined with scars as she handed the baby over.

"You know you could do it part time, weekends or something." Jessie had sidled up beside me, maneuvered me away from the crowd. She passed me a napkin, though I'd barely eaten a bite.

"Yeah, I know," I said. "But Gabby, daycare, and…"

"Danger," she finished for me. "That sister of yours. She put it into your head, didn't she?"

"She's right though."

"Never said she wasn't," Jessie replied, licking frosting off of her finger. "But listen, if you need something in addition to your new desk job, something to keep you from turning into some fat slob of an IT guy, they always need volunteers over in Davis County. I think Haydensboro is close enough that they'd take you. Give 'em a call."

"Volunteer, huh?"

"You could do it, like, once a month. Their call

volume is almost nil, so there's less danger and your sister can get her panties out of a wad. When they do get a call, it's mostly support for the paramedics, maybe a campfire gone a little wild."

"Yeah," I said, pocketing the thought. "Yeah, I'll consider it. But first I need to get my footing with this new life."

She patted my shoulder, leaned in and whispered, "Jed made that cake; you better eat up."

From behind, the captain came up and pulled me into a hug. "We all went in and got a little something for you." He shoved a large box into my hands.

I opened it and lifted the helmet out—inscribed with my name and number.

"You guys," I said, barely able to speak, tipping my head up so I didn't cry, the same way Rachel used to.

"And girls," Jessie added.

"You know what I mean," I said.

And of course they did.

CHAPTER 11

I hold both our spoons—mine and Gabby's—toss them into the air, catching them with opposite hands.

"Add another, Daddy, and it will be juggling," Gabby says, laughing.

"You think I should juggle, huh?" I ask. It reminds me of what I'd said earlier that day to Nora about the circus—me trying to sound clever; and what she'd said back.

"'Course, Daddy."

I flag the waiter, who flies to me on roller skates, then whips another spoon from his apron and twirls away. Gabby is entranced.

"You like this place?" I ask.

"It's amazing," she says.

"Well, wait till you see this." I toss one spoon

in the air, then the other, followed by the third. They crash to the table in an embarrassing clatter and Gabby giggles, hand tight over her mouth, so I can't see the gaps from her two missing teeth.

"Guess I'm not very good at juggling." I collect the spoons just as the waiter arrives with my butterscotch and her cherry chocolate.

"Daddy," she says, dragging my name out in an exaggerated drawl. "If you can't do it at first, you have to practice. That's what Miss Farr says."

"Is that what she says?" I tuck my spoon into a butterscotch swirl, going for as much sugar in my first bite as possible. Gabby is the opposite, eating the cherries, leaving the little squares of chocolate for last.

"'Course."

'Course. Gabby is constantly quoting Miss Farr, her favorite teacher of all time. Young, just out of college with energy and patience for all kinds of cool second grade projects. "What'd you do today?"

"It was the best," Gabby says, digging a moat of ice cream around a cherry chunk.

It's always the best.

Gabby leans forward, like she's telling a secret. "'Course we had to wear masks because it was *science*."

She whispers the word like it's a lot more magic than science.

"Everyone looked so weird with their mouths covered, but Miss Farr said not to worry because you could still see us smiling in our eyes." She demonstrates by covering her mouth and grinning. Sure enough the sides of her eyes wrinkle up. "Can you see it, Daddy?"

"Sure can," I say. I run a finger along the creases and she drops her hand.

"Miss Farr wore a clear plastic mask so we could always see her smile and then she added the baking soda—it's a powder—and do you know what happened, Daddy?"

A cherry sits forlorn and forgotten on her spoon. I lean forward.

"The volcano exploded," she says, whispering the first two words and exploding her own voice at the end.

"Wow," I say, stretching back in my seat.

"It's because a *reaction*." She says each syllable like it's its own word.

"A reaction with what?" I ask, knowing the answer.

"I can't remember," she whispers. "It looked like water. Can we do it at home? Make a volcano?"

"I don't know," I say, smoothing my ice cream

before taking another bite. "If you can't remember the other ingredient."

"I'll remember," she says. "It looked like water, but it wasn't. We smelled it."

"Did it smell like water?"

"Oh no," she says, licking the cherry. "It smelled gross. Romano said it was like throw up."

"That Romano." Gabby talks about him a lot. Ah, second grade.

"I'll find it on YouTube," she says, shoving a big bite of ice cream into her mouth. "The experiment. Then can we do it?"

"Probably," I say. "As long as you find me a video on juggling too, and help me practice."

"'Kay," she says, scraping up the chocolate bits she's saved for last.

"Aren't you hungry?" she asks, looking at my half-full bowl.

Obediently, I tuck my spoon into the softening dessert. "Oh, I'm just thinking," I say.

"About juggling?" she asks.

"Yes," I say, picturing Nora's hair catching the sun as she stood by her bike. "About juggling."

CHAPTER 12

FOUR YEARS EARLIER

J moved out of the master bedroom to a
small room next to Gabby's—the only
other bedroom in the house, and a place where I
could hear her breathe. It became the way I fell
asleep, listening to those breaths. I could count the
length of them, so steady and unburdened.

Six months. She'd drawn dozens of stick figures
of Rachel—the two of them holding hands, the three
of us as a family. One with a round belly that had a
baby in it although we'd told her that wasn't how
she'd come to us. One with a heart between the two
of them. One with a sun and beach, the horizon a
perfect rectangle of solid blue. The pictures became,
for Gabby, the memory themselves. Her mother,
solidified, immortalized in those waxy lines of color.

It was harder for me, with all those years of life

rolling behind me, all the memories of our time together, all those tangles of loss and hurt. More an abstract than a still life.

The new job was a perfect distraction. Codes to master, protocols, clients with their endless flow of computer requests. No doubt I'd lost something in the new security of my job. That was the plan, after all. Lose something to gain it, wasn't that how it went?

The week I took my wedding band off, a waitress at lunch asked me out. Nope, wasn't ready for that. Definitely not what I was missing. I politely declined, put my ring back on. After that, I learned to cook hamburgers and pizza and bacon mac and cheese—all Gabby's favorite foods, as well as a few of my own.

I avoided Rachel's favorites, tried to forget what they were—the cashew chicken, eggplant Parmesan, any pasta at all. It didn't work.

And why hadn't she told me, told me as soon as she knew? A cancer that had leaked to nearly every part of her body. Instead, she'd held the information tight against her. *Protecting you,* she'd said, *working through.* And maybe she'd needed to process it herself, but nothing about it had protected *me.* A selfish thought—*me.* Embarrassing that I could even think of myself when my wife had been the one dying, and yet I had. And once the thought came, it took root, and I struggled to let it go. I found myself constantly wishing that she'd told me right away. As though that would have changed anything, made it different. Still, I wished she'd let me hold her as we cried. Together. Wished she hadn't waited for the follow-up, the surety of the words I'd found in that letter. The letter. If I hadn't found it, when would she have told me? It was a question I never asked her, a question that didn't have an answer that could satisfy me. And so I just wished. That'd I'd been there at the first, with her. A unit, a team.

I didn't resent her for it, wouldn't, couldn't. But I wished. And if ever another woman came along, I promised myself that I would say: "I need you to be honest, even if it hurts." No, not honest—Rachel hadn't lied. *Open.* Open, even if it hurts.

Looking over Gabby's shoulder, I watched her draw a square, choose a red crayon, fill it in, above circles of black for wheels. A fire truck. Another missing thing, but maybe one that I could do something about.

CHAPTER 13

PRESENT

I thumb through the same greasy magazine I'm pretty sure I've picked up every time. It's hard to tell. They all look the same, or maybe they just look the same to me because I'm so distracted.

Nora is helping another customer, while Joe works on my fender—something I haven't even bothered to check the pricing on. If she does wind up with a minute to talk to me, it might turn out to be the most expensive phone number I've ever acquired. I pull out my phone, google bodywork, and suck in a breath.

"Everything okay?" Nora says, sitting down at her desk and filing a receipt away in the neat little system she has for herself.

"Just thinking about how much this is going to cost after labor," I say, not lying.

"Joe'll give you a fair deal, no matter what. Honestly, you're lucky that tire blew so close to here in the first place. Most places would have gouged you, especially if you were in a pinch."

"True enough." Watching her, I definitely feel a little lucky that my tire blew where it did. She moves with a lot of sway—her hair flowing over her shoulders. Her fingers flowing over the papers, body swaying from desk to chair to sales floor. I wonder if she's ever been a dancer.

"So," I begin, as nervous as a teenager. "You seem to like the car stuff too. You always help the customers with the tires."

"Just doing my job," she says.

"Plus a little. I've seen other people man that desk and they never go over the tires and help people as much as you do."

She blushes a little at the comment. Redheads—their complexions always give them away. "I have to admit I do like helping people find just the right thing. Joe's taught me a lot. Brenda too. Have you met her?"

"I did one Saturday, the day I came for my second tire." And now it feels like I'm the one who's blushing.

"Seems like you're kind of getting the full makeover," she says and I sense a bit of her suspicion.

"Well, like you said, it was lucky my tire blew out here." I pray for the front door to not jingle because if someone interrupts, I know I'll lose my nerve. "I got to meet you, after all."

She smiles. It's guarded.

Nobody come in. "Anything else you like besides cars?"

She shrugs.

"Puppies, kittens, small animals of any variety?" I say.

The corner of her mouth tilts up. "Probably more of a lizard person. I've got a gecko in my apartment. They're easier than mammals, and I don't have a lot of spare time."

"I wouldn't have pegged you as a gecko girl."

"Most guys don't."

Uh-oh, starting to feel like dangerous territory again. "My daughter loves lizards too. We get skinks in the yard all summer long and she's always chasing them around."

"Has she caught any?"

"Not yet." I laugh. "They're fast."

"Well, if she's ever here in the summer, I'll teach her a few tricks."

"She'd really like that," I say. "You know, I could get your phone number. Maybe text you about it some time."

Her fingers twitch a little. I see them flutter over the face of her phone. Not sure if it's a good sign or a bad one, but I plow ahead. "Actually, it might be nice to go for coffee or something—you and me. Maybe next time I come down."

"Joe'll get you fixed up; you won't have to be coming down all the time." She looks at the door, like she's hoping someone will come in soon.

But I've come this far, might as well finish it. "I mean, it doesn't have to be for just the car. I could come another day. Maybe Saturday. Is there a good coffee shop around here?"

She swallows. I see it, a visible swallow. Bad sign. "Truthfully..." And there it comes. "I don't usually drink coffee."

"Oh," I say. It seems like a clear enough hint.

But now she's the one who keeps talking. "Makes me jittery."

I nod, ready to bury my head back in the magazine, get my car, and go.

"But I guess I could get an herbal tea or something."

I cock my head to the side, surprised at the turn. "Sure," I say, "But if you don't like coffee, then maybe

—" I'm about to ask her to dinner when she jumps in.

"Actually, there's this really cool chocolate shop in Louisville. Maybe we could drive there and...I mean, that's kind of far, especially for you, never mind."

"No, no," I say, "that's cool. But...doesn't all that sugar make you a little jittery too?" My eyes twinkle at her and I realize that somehow I'm no longer sitting, but standing, right next to the counter as we talk, our faces only a foot or two apart. The freckles make a little map along her nose and I like it.

"I always go dark," she says with a touch of righteousness. "And they've got all these samples. It's fun. I haven't been in years. They call it a chocolate bar." She stops a little abruptly on the last word. "Not a real bar, no drinks or anything."

"I mean, drinks would be cool too. Chocolate and wine," I say.

"Actually, I'm not much of a..."

"...drinker," I finish for her. She pinks up under the freckles, but I smile. "I'm not either. Not since my little girl came along. So chocolate is perfect. Then we can both drive home safely." Now her face is undeniably pink, hot hot pink.

"Actually, I don't have an, um, car. Maybe it's just

too far for you to come here and then go to Louisville."

It's a fire I try to douse. "No, no, drives are fun," I say. *Especially ones with pretty women,* I think. "What time should I pick you up?"

She shakes her head, like she has no idea on time. "Maybe afternoon, so we can get there before it's too late. 4-ish?"

I nod. "That's perfect."

"Here," she says, reaching into a tattered messenger-style purse and pulling out a dingy business card. "This is the address for the chocolate bar. Remy's."

She smiles at the wrinkled card and it seems strange in a world with phones and Google that that's how she keeps the address. I take a picture of it with my phone. "And your address?" I ask. "Maybe that phone number too."

"Oh, yeah," she says, her hands shaking a bit.

She gives me her number, her address, and then we look at each other for one awkward second. This is when I should make my grand exit, but I've still got to get my car back.

"Saturday," I say.

"It'll be fun," she adds.

Fortunately we're both saved by Joe, who comes out, wiping his hands in that way he does. "Turns out your fender wasn't so bad after all," he says. "Just a couple bangs to get that dent out and you're good to go. Hope it didn't waste your time, you driving all the way down here."

"Wasn't a waste at all," I say, giving Nora a slight sideways glance, which she skillfully ignores, all business now that Joe is back in the room.

"Glad to hear it," Joe says, and then the trademark wink.

This weekend. My first date (barring one horrible thing I don't think could rightly be called a date) since Rachel. I feel a little sick to my stomach, but not in a flu virus way, more in a waiting-in-line-for-a-roller-coaster way. It's been a while.

CHAPTER 14

FOUR YEARS EARLIER

"*D*avis County," Jessie said. "I'll text you the number."

"I don't want to have anything really serious," I added, feeling twitchy about calling. "Going into buildings and all that."

"Yeah, yeah," she said. "Honestly, you'll be lucky to have them call you in for anything out in Davis. There isn't a lot going on. When you do get called, it's usually to help the medics with a lift assist."

"Glamorous," I said.

"They always need help with the big ones."

I could hear her smiling over the phone. None of us loved list assists, especially when the patient was heavy enough to need four people, not two. But by volunteering here and there, I'd be back with my people, helping out, even if it was just to help get a heavy patient on the cot and out to an ambulance. "Sounds great," I said, and hung up the phone.

***

*I*t wasn't a lift assist.

For my first call as a volunteer firefighter, I found myself on the scene of a raging fire. Dispatch had radioed it out as an illegal burn. Simple enough—usually a campfire or someone burning trash. But this, this was a drunken bonfire, which spread through a narrow field of dry corn stalks, catching the decrepit farmhouse beside it. Most of the people were out of the house, reveling as they'd been, but one of the men—scruffy beard, squinting eyes—he was sobbing like a baby, repeating, "You've got to get her out."

"Who, sir?" I asked.

"My grandma. She always takes a Tylenol PM and ain't nothing can wake her. She's dead asleep upstairs."

Dead asleep. I thought it a poor choice of words, but called to the other firefighters who were gallantly spraying the sides of the house that I was going to go in.

Why had I done it? Why had I basically volunteered to be the one running in? Plenty of logical reasons popped up. Old habits kicked in; the other volunteers were busy; as the "newbie" I'd been left to take a report and it had turned into more than that—there hadn't been a lot of time for deliberation. Plus, fires were loud—wild, roaring things, water sprayed at high velocity, the elements battling it out for dominance. It didn't leave room for chitchat.

Besides, the scene looked safe, the walls still stable, the temperature reasonable, only the western side of the house was actually on fire. I went in the East door, the screen swinging haphazardly on its hinges. On this side of the house, the smoke wasn't thick, though you could smell it, like every burned meal in the world had combined into the farmhouse foyer. I put my mask on, went up the narrow staircase to the floor where the man had said the bedrooms were.

The fire hadn't even reached this high yet, but fires liked to creep up walls, sometimes race up walls. Unless the other firefighters had stopped it. I opened the first door, then the second. I began to wonder if the drunken grandson knew what he was talking about, but at the third I found her—just as the man had said—asleep. Looking at her, she did look dead. I hoped she wasn't. I moved to the bed, shook her aggressively. She moaned, which I appreciated. "Ma'am," I said. Then not knowing how to finish, I added, "It's time to wake up." She only turned in response. I shook her again, putting my arms under her back and lifting her up to a sitting position. She kept her eyes closed, like a stubborn child who didn't want to get up for school.

I was trying not to drag her—old bodies don't handle it particularly well and she'd probably wind up bruised and maybe even with a broken bone or two, and I knew I couldn't lift her. Despite the Hollywood image of a firefighter gallantly carrying children and gorgeous woman from the belly of a fire, this woman wasn't a size that could be easily hoisted into my arms, or even over my shoulder.

"Up we go," I said, using my legs to heave her into a standing position.

Finally, she opened her eyes. "What are you doing in my house?" she asked, adding an impressive curse.

"Well, ma'am," I said, glancing down at my coat. "Your house is currently on fire."

"Those boys," she said, cursing again, but stumbling forward now, gripping my forearms with long fingernails.

"Careful now," I said, starting down the stairs. It should have gotten cooler with each step, but I swore they all felt every bit as hot. Sweat was pouring down my face, dripping into my eyes. The woman stumbled and we both nearly rolled to the bottom, but I held tightly to the rail until she found her footing.

We could hear the fire now and she held a sleeve up to her nose. There was a lot more smoke than when I'd come up these stairs. Instinctively, we both crouched down, trying to get beneath the gray smoke to the door. Even the floor was hot as we touched it. "Ima kill 'em," she said. We moved to our hands and knees, a steady crawl.

Outside, one of the walls cracked—a sound like thunder. She screamed and stopped moving.

"It's okay," I said. "Keep moving. We're just about there."

"My house," she said, her voice hoarse from smoke and emotion.

I could feel the air from the door, the cool breeze leading us like a trail of bread crumbs. And then the breeze slammed it closed.

The old woman swore again. I stood, hunched over and jogged forward, opening the door. "This way," I said, reaching a hand out and helping her to stand up. Outside, the cold slapped our faces and she took a sharp breath of the sweet air.

Standing in her yard, we looked around. Gray smoke billowed against the black night sky, swirling in patterns above our heads. Half of the house seemed to drip, black and charred, though the flames were receding now, losing their battle with the hoses. She lifted a hand to her eyes, started to cry.

I wrapped an arm around her as a medic came over to check her vitals and help her into the ambulance. "I haven't even worn a robe," she blubbered. "On a cold night like this."

"Oh, we've seen much worse than that nightgown," the medic said, smiling. "Least you thought to get dressed before bed." He helped her to the stretcher.

I stood for just a moment, taking it all in, the woman in the ambulance, the house of blackened charcoal, tiles and chunks of wood fallen and smoking on the ground.

The grandson tripped over to the ambulance, crying. "You saved her." He hugged me and I smelled the alcohol and sweat and relief.

I had. Saved an old woman. Given her back to her family. A moment of joy, of ecstasy really. One we rarely got.

But it had been dangerous. Controlled as much as things like fire could be controlled. In other words: not very controlled. I knew I should stop volunteering after this, hang up my hat, call it an amazing life experience—those years I'd served. Served. Past tense. But I also knew that I wouldn't. Even though I worried about getting hurt or even killed. Even though I worried about leaving Gabby behind.

I wandered back to the truck, took my mask off, feeling for the first time in my life like I was having an affair.

CHAPTER 15

PRESENT

*W*hat does a guy wear for his first first date in fifteen years? A suit seems like way too much. Business casual screams golfing, not chocolate bar. I let the idea of a chocolate bar roll around it my head, the sound of it, the feel, try to picture what people will be wearing.

I drag out a pair of dark jeans, a little on the skinny side, but not too much. Rachel liked these. I shove them back in, settle on a baggier bluer pair, a nice shirt. It looks good, I think, but how can I know? I always used to ask Rachel if she liked what I was wearing. I button the shirt, shake my head. Maybe it's a colossally bad idea, this date, but I can dress myself; I've been doing it for years. I'm just surprisingly nervous. One of the best things about getting married was that I was never supposed to have to do this again—this slightly nauseous feeling, this worry about clothes and addresses, this feeling of discomfort.

I check the mirror, mostly satisfied. My eyes settle on my shoes. Except for my IT interview, I haven't thought about what shoes to wear in three years. I switch my tennis shoes out for a pair of black loafers and feel like it's not quite perfect, but decent. Rachel would approve. I try to push her out of my mind and then feel guilty about trying to push her out of my mind.

Gabby shows up at my door. I've only told her I'm going out with a friend. Is she old enough yet to read between the lines? Does it matter if she is? "You look nice, Daddy."

Kate rings the bell and I'm relieved that that's where the conversation ends.

I've told Kate I'm going out with a friend too, but as soon as I answer the door, she gives me a quick glance and quirks an eyebrow up. My sister can definitely read between the lines, but she doesn't comment. "Hey, Gabs," she says, swooping Gabby up in a hug. "You ready for a day with the boys?"

"Are the lizards still out?" she asks and I think about Nora and her gecko.

"A couple of them, lying in the sun. Easier to catch this time of year."

Gabby smiles.

"Well, *I'm* ready for a day with a girl," Kate continues.

Gabby giggles.

"After you're done catching lizards with Luke and Nathan, we can do our nails and bake some cookies."

"What kind?" Gabby asks, squirming into her jacket.

"What kind do you want?" Kate asks.

"Double chocolate," Gabby says, without a second's pause.

I must look strange because Kate looks at me again. "Why do you look guilty?" she asks.

"I'm not guilty," I say.

"I didn't say you were," she says, "only that you look it."

"Daddy's got a date," Gabby whispers. So apparently, she can read between the lines too. Girls learn that pretty young. Pretty sure I wouldn't have figured it out till I was thirty.

"Is that so?" Kate asks. "Well, I hope he has a good time." Another look.

"Got to go," I say, leaning over to kiss Gabby, then giving Kate a squeeze. "Thanks, Katie."

"My pleasure," Kate says. "I really do need some girl time. I should probably steal this lady every

Saturday." A pointed look in my direction. "Otherwise, with all that boy time, I might start thinking fart jokes are actually funny."

Gabby laughs like she thinks fart jokes are very funny indeed.

"Everyone knows fart jokes *are* funny," I say, opening the door to the garage and letting one rip.

"Ugh," both Kate and Gabby squeal, running for the front door.

"You better get that out of your system before your *date,*" Kate hollers at me and Gabby laughs, like they're *both* my older sisters.

I hear the front door slam, and head to my car, still smiling. Seeing the car, sitting a little lackluster in the garage, I start to worry that I should have had it cleaned.

First dates.

It's been a while.

CHAPTER 16

FOUR-THREE-TWO-ONE YEARS EARLIER

*S*econd volunteer firefighter call: lift assist, just like Jessie said. Four hundred pounder.

*F*irst broken arm—Gabby, not me. She was only four and she'd banged it on a monkey bar, that's all. When we got to the orthopedist, I asked him to check for bone density and other problems, considering her history. Gabby looked at me, confused at the word, the concept of medical history.

· · ·

*T*hird call: Abandoned car. Someone who drove by it called to make sure no one was inside. No one was.

*G*abby asked about her bio mother—though she called her her belly mother. She wanted to know her name. I didn't know. Her hair color. I didn't know. Her eye color. Didn't know. Anything at all. She was beautiful, I told her, because she brought us *you.*

"But she left me," Gabby said, sorting through the supplies we'd bought her for kindergarten in the fall.

"She left because she couldn't care for you and needed to find someone who could."

Gabby didn't bring it up again. Didn't draw pictures, didn't play with her animals and use them to act out her problems.

*F*ourth call: Fire alarm, false alarm.

*F*ifth call: Fire alarm, false alarm.

. . .

*S*ixth call: Fire alarm, school. False alarm. Child suspended. I felt bad for him.

*F*irst day of kindergarten. Gabby cried and cried like I hadn't even known she could. She refused to let go of my arm, even when I tried to pry her fingers off, even when her teacher showed her the desk with the lollipop wrapped in a ribbon. I stayed for several minutes, then snuck out of the room. Four steps down the hall, I heard her wailing begin. I stopped, wondered if I should return, then left. My head bowed, tears burning the backs of my own eyes.

*S*eventh call: Security alarm, false alarm.

*G*abby cried every day. She started waking in a night sweat, crying, swinging her arms. One night, she punched my nose, leaving a small bruise. I called the school therapist, who referred me to another therapist.

First therapist appointment. Several medicines available. Did I want to try them?

Well, did I?

I flipped through the scrapbooks Rachel created, wondering why she had to leave me alone when she knew I needed her. Clicked off my light, closed my eyes.

Gabby woke screaming. My own eyes flashed open and we began the night.

*E*ighth call: Life Alert button, false alarm.

*H*alfway through kindergarten, Gabby stopped crying. Started wetting the bed. I agreed to try medicine. It didn't help.

*N*inth call: Lift assist. Three hundred pounder.

*T*herapist diagnosis: Anxiety. Feels a little broad.

. . .

*T*enth call: Heart attack. He was dead by the time we got there to help the medics.

*S*ummer at the beach. Scrapbooks. Seashells. Gabby kept the bed dry. We watched the clouds roll in, made spaghetti and corn dogs for dinner, ate too much ice cream.

*E*leventh call: Oven fire. Out in five minutes.

*G*abby found a kitten (only a few weeks old) under the tree in the backyard. Its back was scratched and bloody; its fur dirty. I found Gabby under the tree, feeding it milk by dipping her finger into a dish and then letting it suck the liquid off. I called the humane society. We could foster it, they told us. That afternoon, I stopped by for supplies, including a small bottle and a container of flea medicine. "I don't know if we can keep it, baby girl," I said.

"Why not?" she asked, tipping the bottle into the

tiny mouth like she'd been caring for kittens her whole life.

Because it's another fragile thing to care for, I thought, and said, "What if she scratches the furniture or gets fleas or you're allergic?" *What if she dies,* I also thought.

And then Gabby said, "It's like me. The mother left her here because she couldn't take care of her, but we can."

We named her Moxie.

*T*welfth call: Medics called us to break open a door when they couldn't get into the house they were dispatched to. Woman wandered out in a robe. 911 butt dial apparently. Got cussed out.

*F*irst grade. No tears. No tantrums. Dry bed. Moxie slept by Gabby's head, sometimes with a paw across her face. In the morning, Gabby woke with both cat hair and her own hair sticking out at angles from her forehead. Occasionally, she sneezed a lot, but no one cared. When the weather cooled we all three sat on the heater vent, wrapped in a blanket that billowed from the stream of warm air.

CHAPTER 17

PRESENT

I don't bring flowers, don't even think about it till I'm at her door. It would have been nice. Rachel would have liked it. I push the thought away. Flowers are too intense anyway for this date that was supposed to be just coffee.

She comes to the door in a floor-length sundress, bright orange flowers sprouting across it, a light sweater over her arms, hair twisted into some type of knot I could never correctly name. "You look nice," I say, feeling again like I should have something to hand her across the threshold. Her apartment is a tiny thing. Not studio. Somewhere inside I hear music playing.

She sees that I hear it. "My roommate," she says, and I nod, surprised. It's not that it's a bad thing for her to have a roommate, just unexpected, something I haven't had since my firefighter training. Suddenly, I hope I haven't asked out a nineteen-year-old.

"Should we go?" It's an awkward sentence, for that awkward moment of that awkward thing that is a first date. The awkwardness, I realize, even shines from both of our outfits, carefully chosen. From our scrubbed faces, clean nails. She steps past me, an awareness of me watching, though I'm also aware and trying not to watch. As she moves out of her door, I notice that she smells nice, too. Not floral, but spicy, like fall. Maybe the awkwardness is worth it.

I hurry down the stairs and grab her door. She slips in, seemingly unaware that I haven't had the car washed in ages, moves the kid sunglasses from the seat.

"Oh, sorry about that."

"They're cute," she says. "I'm sure they look great on you." She smiles, and it's nice. I feel my shoulders start to relax.

As I walk around the car, I tap in the address for the chocolate bar. It brings up a name that isn't Remy's, a place that looks more like a burger joint than a chocolate shop. I don't know why, but I don't mention it to her when I get in the car. I figure we'll wind up where we wind up and work it out from there. Maybe one of the numbers is off. No biggie.

I should have mentioned it.

She stands in front of the restaurant like a patient in shock. I touch her shoulder gently, trying to nudge her out of it. "So…" I say. "Burgers?"

She attempts a smile, but it's crooked. A smile I've seen before on women when they're trying not to cry, like their lipstick got a little melty.

"Probably just got a number of the address off," I say. "Or maybe it's South instead of North. Should we drive down the street and look for it?"

"No," she says, her voice a little crooked too. She clears her throat. "This is the place. I recognize the building, and that empty lot over there. I guess I just didn't think to check if Remy's was still here."

I walk to the door and she freezes. "Well," I say, stopping. "We could get a burger; maybe they even have good chocolate shakes."

"Not sure how I could have done something so stupid," she says, still not stepping forward.

I shrug. "We've all done stuff like that."

"Who doesn't think to check something like

that?" she says, and this time, it's like she's talking to herself and not to me.

"Chocolate shakes?" I prod.

She snaps herself out of it. "Sure, if you're hungry." She smiles, but it's the type of smile that looks like she's trying to be brave, not like she really wants to go in.

And here I find myself confronted with a choice —a choice I haven't made since marriage, a choice I haven't always made correctly. 1) Ignore that wobbly smile, go in, get some food, probably have a decent time. 2) Pay attention, see what she wants to do, maybe find out why.

"Or we could go somewhere else."

Her smile relaxes. "Sure, that could be fun."

"It could," I say, looking at her.

"There's a museum," she adds. "I don't think it's far."

I nod and then she laughs. "Of course I haven't exactly proven myself super trustworthy in the memory department, so maybe we should check."

I pull out my phone. This time, she's nailed it. A sculpture museum is just a few miles away. I click the map on my phone. "Done," I say. "Let's go."

"If you really had your heart set on food," she adds, casting a backward glance at the burger place, "we could go."

I don't think *I* was the one with my heart set on something, but I don't say that. "Nah. This will be fun." Though I'm not sure I've ever gone to an art museum, much less a *sculpture* museum, in my life.

The sculptures increase in size as you go through. They start, seriously, with ones as small as your fingernail, and just keep growing.

"They're made from things around the city," she tells me. "Junk." We both pause to gaze at a giraffe made from coffee cans, rusty trowels, and broken terra cotta pots. The plaque titles it, "Savanna Regrown."

"Where do people get the junk?" I ask, walking slightly closer, catching her gingery scent in the breezes of our movement.

"Well, a lot of it is found items," she says and I nod like this isn't a new, artsy concept to me. "And at this point, the city will often donate things. Builders and people will call the museum and offer the stuff they have, see if any of the artists can use it."

"And can they?" I ask.

She shrugs. "I'm sure there's too much trash in a city this size for it to all get used, but it's still a nice gesture and provides the artists with plenty of free materials."

"I take it you've been here more recently than the chocolate bar." For a minute, I think it was a mistake, to bring up the wrong place thing again, but then she smiles.

"Good observation. I haven't been to Remy's since I was a kid—eleven or so maybe, but I started coming here on the weekends about a year ago. They change out some of the art every month, so I would take the bus the first Saturday of every month. At least I did for about six months. Then life got busy."

"Busy?" I ask.

"Yeah," she says as we look at a replica of Godzilla made entirely from bolts. "I started school—night classes."

"Cool," I say. "What are you studying?"

"Well, right now it's just general ed stuff."

She didn't answer the question. I don't press.

A cityscape rises up on one wall. I cock my head to the side, trying to figure out what city it is. She does a similar thing. "It's not Louisville," she says.

"Not New York either," I add.

"Chicago?" I ask.

"No idea," she says.

The plaque doesn't even bother to give us a hint, which makes me wonder if it's a real city at all.

Whatever it is, it's made from plastic—bottles of all sorts, yogurt containers, grocery bags, vegetables wrappings. All melted and soldered together into a bumpy mass of buildings. It's labeled simply, "Consume."

"Well, that's cheerful," I say.

"At least it's not made from dead sea turtles," she adds. "Though we definitely consume too much. Maybe I should rethink my candy jar."

"No," I say with mock melodrama.

She laughs and our hands brush as we walk through the double doors leading to the outdoor gardens.

"So, hold on," I say, thinking about candy. "Even though you've come here so much and it's close to where Remy's was, you never stopped off at the chocolate bar?"

She shrugs. "It's better with people and I always came here alone. So...no, I guess I didn't."

I taste the slightest hint of smoke in her words, not for me, but for something else. There's a story under it, a fire about to light, but she's not willing to drop the match.

"Look at this," she says. An enormous bicycle made from abandoned and broken bicycles rises up almost a story above our heads.

"Whoa."

"The best part is on the other side," she adds, taking my arm and pulling me around. Her hand isn't exactly soft—the tips of the fingers a little rough, and I notice that they're a little knobby, but they've got a solid, strong feel that I can't help but enjoy.

At the rear of the enormous sculpture is a ladder you can climb to the top.

"Is it stable?" I ask.

"I've gone up every time." She gathers up her dress, tightening it around her legs, and begins to climb.

At the top, the sculptor has positioned several old bike seats so that people can sit. Nora settles down and I follow suit, out legs dangling over the edge. Below us a few other people wander through the sculpture garden. "I'm surprised more people don't come here," I say.

"Yeah," she responds. "It deserves more attention, but I have to admit that one of the things I like about it is that it doesn't get too many people. Which is selfish of me, now that I'm saying it out loud. "

"Makes sense though," I reply. "It's a good place to think."

"What are you thinking about?" she asks.

The honest truth is that I'm feeling more things right now than I'm thinking, and all those feelings are clumped together in a confusing way, so I lie. Well, sort of. I guess it must be one of the things I'm thinking since I come up with it. "Just thinking about how you said you're taking classes at night. What for?"

"English, Math, general ed," she says.

"That's what you said earlier, but what's your aim, or are you just learning to learn or something?"

"Well, that would be cool of me, but no," she says. "I guess long-game, I'd like to be an engineer."

I'm not sure why it surprises me with the car shop and all, but something about the dress, full of orange flowers, the museum, the love affair with a chocolate bar—I'd pinned her as an artist. And in a moment of candor, I say so.

"But don't you see," she laughs. "Engineering is art. It's putting things together to create something new. The only difference is that the art of engineering has function, not just form."

The sun has just started to get serious about setting—its color deepening as it fattens, sinking through the clouds. The clouds seem to part for the sun, pinking up on one side. And for a minute, I'm amazed at the serendipity of it. Here we are sitting on an enormous bike watching the sun drop through candied clouds, when we had been planning to stuff our faces with chocolate all night long. "I'm sorry about Remy's," I say. "But I'm really glad we came here."

"It is pretty amazing," she replies, and for several minutes we just sit there, neither of us saying anything. Was it just a few hours ago that I was worrying about flowers and awkward hellos? It seems impossible. Our heads tip toward each other, and I almost think she is going to lean her cheek on my shoulder when the intercom blares. "The museum will be closing in fifteen minutes. Please make your way to the nearest exit."

"Oh, yeah," she says with a sigh. "They close early on Saturday, so they can host events."

"I guess they've got to make money somehow," I reply.

Neither of us moves to make our way to the nearest exit though. The sun sags against the horizon. The clouds flare like someone lit them on fire— red and orange and living. "They're like flames," I say.

"Capturing the light," she adds.

Her hand is close to mine and I almost take it when a couple walks beneath us, the sun sinks another inch, and the clouds dull.

"We better go," she says. "Don't want to upset the security guy. He's real cranky." She smiles a little wickedly, and for the first time, I hear a little deep Kentucky in her accent and wonder which part of the state she's from.

"Ladies first," I say.

"No, you go. You're closer and I'll have to scooch in front of you. It won't be very lady-like either way."

I shimmy down the ladder as quickly as I can.

"Wow," she says. "You're like a spider or something."

"Yeah, well, ladders and I have a history."

She doesn't ask what I mean. She's too focused on wrapping the dress around her legs and making her way down. "This outfit seemed like a better idea when I thought we'd be eating chocolate."

"Well, who knew we'd spend the evening climbing a building-sized bicycle?" I ask.

Her foot slips on a rung near the bottom, and I reach up to hold her waist. "You good?" I ask.

"Yeah," she says, hopping over the final rung and landing nicely on her feet, just a few inches from me. It makes me sweat. The intercom buzzes again. "Five minutes until closing. Please find the nearest door and exit the building."

"Uh-oh," I say, grabbing her hand before I think

about it—it's just what I would have done with Gabby, but so different. "Better run."

We hurry back into the building and out a side door with a big arrow pointing to it. When we reach the parking lot, I'm still holding her hand, and she only just seems to notice. We hold the position in a little freeze, back to a bit of awkwardness, now with a bit of heat; and then her strong fingers lace through mine, committing to the hold.

"You up for a some food?" I ask, then quickly add, "Not at the burger place; somewhere else."

"Sure," she says. "How long have you got your sitter?"

For a second, I don't know what she means. "Oh, Gabby. Well, the sitter is my sister, so...long enough for some food."

She smiles and I notice again how straight her teeth are, how white and square. I lean in, just a little. Too straight. The two top teeth have been replaced. I want to ask her what happened—some accident as a kid maybe. I personally chipped one of mine once on a call, so I know the look. But I also know it would embarrass Nora if I ask, mortify her that I noticed. So I walk to the car, touching her waist just once to point her in the right direction.

I'm surprised at the end of the night when she ends up with a vanilla shake, not a drop of chocolate anywhere. Maybe the loss of Remy's is still a little too close.

She leaves me that night, not with a kiss, but a sweet, sideways hug. I pull her in all the way. Warm, soft curves connected to the rest of her angular, muscular body. A heat rises up my center. I pull back, swallowing. "I'd really like to call you again," I say.

"I'd really like to answer."

INTERLUDE

NORA

What a crazy thing not to check. Whether your place of childhood utopia still exists. Of course, it would exist because removing it would be like removing the mother who brought you life.

So, yeah, I should have assumed it was gone.

I won't tell a story of how I grew up with my mama and daddy and things were good until my mama died and then Daddy took to drinking.

Things were never fine. And Daddy could be plenty mean with or without drinking. My mama left before I could remember her being there.

And then one day she came back.

I arrived home from school in fourth grade and there, perched at the edge of the smoking chair that was usually my dad's, was a woman. Straight as a flagpole, hair a yellow line to her waist, lipstick drawn in a smooth red rose around her lips. "Hey, baby doll," she said, standing up and clutching a purse that matched her lips precisely. "I'm your mama, and I'm taking you for chocolate."

Daddy just lay on the couch, looking sullen, but not resisting. When I glanced at him, he nodded. And so I went. Put a hand into the hand she offered and drove to the center of Louisville with a woman I hadn't met within memory.

It's not hard to fall in love though. Not with a beautiful woman over chocolate. A woman who holds your hand and coos with an accent not quite Kentucky and certainly not country like mine was, but deep, dignified south. We ate truffles and turtles and nonpareils.

Then, at the end of the day, over chocolate splits (no bananas need apply), we broke up.

"I won't be seeing you again, sweetie."

I looked up, licked the sticky ridges at the corners of my mouth. "I'm sorry, ma'am."

What else was I supposed to say?

"I'm not your ma'am. I'm your mama. But, sweetie, I'm very sick. The doctor told me last week."

Now I'd been sick before and this woman didn't look sick to me. I watched the red lips. All that chocolate and the lipstick hadn't even smudged.

I didn't cry, but I didn't finish my ice cream

either.

On the way out, she reached up to the counter, handed me an Andes Mint and a business card. Remy's. I said the store name three times, feeling the smooth line of the 'e,' held in by the melty consonants—a truffle of a word.

Then she took my hand and drove me home.

I didn't see her again. Didn't hear from her. Maybe she died. Maybe she didn't. In my mind I can see her eyes—a pop of blue, the red lips never changing. Maybe that's how she wanted it—that permanently beautiful woman. Or maybe I just hadn't noticed the way that her cheeks were too pale. Or that when she lifted a slim hand to take a bite, her fingers shook. Maybe the creamy soft cardigan was there to cover bone-skinny arms instead of making a fashion statement. I'll never know. In my eyes, she'd been perfect. And then she'd left. Like perfect things did.

My father never told me anything about her—not her life, not her death. I realized a few years later that I didn't even know her name.

But I did keep that slip of paper, the business card from Remy's; and I thought that maybe one day when the time was right I'd go back.

I guess the time wasn't right.

I guess it wouldn't ever be.

CHAPTER 18

THREE YEARS EARLIER

There *had* been one other first date about a year after Rachel's death, a night I tried not to think about.

She'd been good looking. I'd give her that. This first and only other date, this woman who'd said her name was Audrey, though I later learned that it was Mary. Audrey hadn't even been a middle name, just a piece of fantasy. Much like the idea that we would have ever worked out.

I wouldn't have started with the buxom new secretary, except that a couple of the IT guys were pushing me. And, sure, it'd been a year. I didn't know what I had to lose.

A night of my life and over $400—nearly two days' salary, that's what I had to lose.

I took her to a hotel in downtown Louisville for

dinner. It was something I'd never done with Rachel and that's what attracted me to the idea. The thought of going anywhere I'd been with my wife—any of the sweet little haunts or dull little normalcies—horrified me. So we wound up in a velvety bar ordering drinks. I got a beer, four times as expensive as it would have been anywhere else. She started with a cocktail—a dark pink at the bottom that ascended into a cotton candy and completed its journey in a gentle slushy blush, which was topped with whipped cream and pink sprinkles. I don't know why it fascinated me so much—these children's delicacies on the top of a grown-up woman's adult beverage, but I couldn't stop looking at those sprinkles. She pounded through the drink in about five minutes, ate the sprinkles and cream with a spoon, and ordered another. Nerves, maybe—I tried to give her that. She wanted to relax. I did too. It'd been a long week at work, and she was the new girl. It couldn't have been easy, though I wasn't sure it was three-cocktails-in-the-first-hour hard. Her laughter cranked higher each time the drink sank to the bottom and I looked at the bartender, desperate for a way to stop the insanity. I'd still only had a few sips of my beer. I pushed the rest away and led my date, already thoroughly tipsy, to a table for two where she ordered a bottle of wine and shrimp hors d'oeuvres. I asked for extra bread, not caring if it made me look like a hillbilly. I was hoping that if she got some food in her system, it might slow her down.

"So," I opened, trying to continue our conversation from the bar. "How are you liking the job?"

"It's my fourth in nine months," she gushed, leaning forward. She'd chosen a tight cherry red dress that I had to admit hugged beautifully in all the right places, but I found myself looking away, over to the waiter, then back into her eyes, hoping to find something there that didn't feel like glass.

"Wow," I said. "Looking for the right thing I guess?"

She took another gulp of wine. "Temp jobs," she said. "I keep bumping up against harassment cases."

I definitely looked away now, though she didn't seem to notice.

"Oh, not like you," she said. "This is nice, so nice." She smiled, her teeth a little stained from the wine, though I could tell they were beautiful, that she was beautiful. On the outside anyway, maybe even on the inside too—I didn't know—because all that beauty was starting to blur into a night I just wanted to escape.

"I'm sorry that's happened to you," I said, tightening my tie, buttoning my jacket.

She shrugged. "Par for the course. Women in the workplace and all."

I pulled my eyebrows together. She was talking like it was 1962. I thought about Jessie, about Katie, about Rachel and her dental practice. I pushed the last thought away. Audrey popped another shrimp into her mouth.

"And what is it you want to do?" I asked. "For a job? If you could…" I gestured at nothing, not knowing how to end the sentence. "…get away from the harassment."

"I always wanted to own my own yoga studio, to be honest," she said. "Think I'm too curvy for it though." She ran both hands down the sides of the tight dress.

"No, you'd be great at it."

"Probably wouldn't," she said, giggling. "I don't even do yoga."

I didn't know what to say, couldn't tell if it was a joke, if I was the joke. Something was a joke, but I wasn't getting it. I made desperate eyes at the waiter, hoping he would hurry the food along and end this night for me as quickly as possible.

He wasn't quick enough. She'd ordered a second bottle of wine and regaled me with dozens of stories of other dates before I managed to plow my way through half my entrée. My own wineglass sat

119

almost untouched. As she finished the last few drops of her wine, she looked at my full glass. Looked at it like she wanted to scoot it to her side of the table. I waved for the check—something I'd never done in my life. The waiter brought it and my breath caught at all the numbers on that slim piece of paper. Neat rows of too much money. But it was okay. Within an hour, I'd be home, tucking Gabby in. Then I could forget all about this night.

Walking to the lobby, I helped her into her coat, or tried to. Her high heels slipped on one of the tiles and she stumbled, grabbing onto the edge of a counter, where a blue and gold vase toppled and then crashed—hundreds of porcelain splinters screaming through the quiet room. A maitre d' or someone rushed over to help. She righted herself, coat still only half on, and then swore at him. He stepped back, straightened his own coat. "Ma'am, if you would please lower your voice."

And then she yelled. Something about how dumb it was to keep precious things in the lobby of a nice hotel like this. I don't know. The whole thing blurred together into a white flash that I blocked somehow. We were asked by someone at some point to leave. I gave them my credit card at some point for the vase (which I really hoped was a Hobby Lobby special). I ushered her out and she gestured at me, saying something about her boyfriend—then a moment when I realized she meant me.

The valet brought out her car first, but I couldn't possibly let her drive it home. "Uh," I said to the valet. "Can you take it back, park it for the night; she's not really..." She vomited on the curb like she'd been waiting for the cue all night.

The valet stepped back. "It will be $40/night," he said.

"I'll pay for the first night," I said, reaching into my coat for my wallet. No credit card this time. I was grateful that my dad had told me to always bring a little cash on a first date. I handed the valet two twenties. She could come get it, or they could impound the car, but I wouldn't be charged again.

They brought my car out shortly after as Audrey was trying to reapply her lipstick—something she did surprisingly well considering how much she swayed on her feet. "You know," I said, looking at my car, which had been freshly washed for the night. "Let me get you an Uber or something." I opened up the app on my phone. "What's your address?" She slurred out an answer and I looked at the valet, who simply raised both eyebrows. She handed me her purse and I popped it open, looking for a driver's license or checkbook. Strike and strike. She had neither. Just a tube of lipstick, a bit of perfume, some birth control pills, and a bottle of prescription of Topamax for migraines, which is where I found her real name. Mary Steele. And the address where I sent her once the Uber arrived.

When I finally got home, I asked Kate to stay the night.

"Why?" she asked, picking up her keys, like she was going to ignore me.

"I want an alibi in case that woman brings up any harassment charges at work. I want someone to be able to say I was home when I was home. I already asked for the valet at the hotel to vouch for me there."

Kate plopped her hands onto her hips. "Surely it wasn't that bad."

"Surely it was."

She looked at my tight noose of a tie, my jacket buttoned, my shoes with just a touch of vomit on one toe. Set her keys and phone down. "I miss Rachel," she said then. And pulled me—her little brother who towered over her—in for a hug.

I didn't cry; I was still wound too tight for it.

"Go get a shower," Katie said. "I'm gonna stream that new Marvel series, and you're going to watch it with me."

"I've got to get to sleep," I said.

"For what?" she asked.

"You know how early Gabby wakes up in the morning."

"I know you won't sleep in the state you're in anyway, so you should do something to relax."

I fell asleep on the couch halfway through the second episode. I found Kate already up in the morning, making her famous peanut butter oatmeal with chocolate chips. Gabby plunked on my wrinkled pajama lap and scraped at the scruff along my chin with her fingernails. The sun rested in squares all along the table and chairs, catching Gabby's blond hair and turning it gold. Going on another date didn't seem like something I would ever need to do again.

Every piece of family I needed was here.

CHAPTER 19

PRESENT

I show up at Nora's work. Kind of a spontaneous thing, especially for me. I don't really have the day off, but I'm working remotely today and it seemed...like a fun thing to do. I shake my head as I park the car. I don't even have an excuse on hand. All new tires, and the car is running perfectly. I'm careful to arrive early enough that she won't be off for lunch yet, and I'm pleased to see her bike locked to a post.

I finger the chocolate bar I brought her. I'd been planning to slip it into the bike basket, but suddenly it seems a little too silly, a little too mushy. I leave it in my car.

The bell jingles when I walk through. She looks up, that moment of recognition—it's the part I'm most worried about. And then she smiles. Those white teeth, pink lips. She's got some kind of gloss on today and it looks good against her skin. "Another problem with your car?" she asks. "I thought Joe had that thing up and running."

"He does," I say. "Never better. I guess I just stopped by hoping you hadn't had your lunch yet and we could go somewhere." I hear the false ring in my own words—*dropped by*, as though I live down the street, *hadn't gone to lunch yet*—it's just ten o'clock. I wait for her to feel those details too. And she does. The air thickens a little between us. Maybe I should have broken something in my car.

"Yeah, sure, maybe," she says, all in quick succession. "I don't get my lunch till eleven though, so it'll be a bit of a wait, and I'm supposed to go get the sandwiches today. We take turns, the guys and I, picking up lunch."

"Right," I say, then realize I've said it too loudly and lower my voice. "I'll just head to the coffee shop down the street, get some of my work done. At eleven I'll come and get you. We can eat, and then get the sandwiches for the guys. Is that okay?"

"Yeah, okay." It's still a little guarded, or maybe something else. Whatever it is, I can feel it. I'm really glad I didn't slip the chocolate bar into her bike basket.

"If you, um, don't have time today, that's okay

too," I say. "I'm working remotely, so just thought I'd come down."

"No, it's good," she says, her voice opening up, like a bit of sun just broke through a cloud. "It's nice."

My phone goes off and I motion awkwardly to it. It's one of our clients and I step outside, walking one of our smaller clients through the ins and outs of the website we've created. By the time I'm done, it's nearly eleven and I don't have time to go to the coffee shop, so I walk around the block, finishing up another call just in time to meet Nora out front. She's smoothing her jeans. The air has gotten cooler, she doesn't have a sweater, and her arms have goosebumps up and down them. I reach out to touch a spot near her elbow where a rose winds along her skin. She jerks back.

"Oh, sorry," I say, stuffing my hands into my pockets.

"No, no problem," she answers. "It's a new tattoo. Kind of tender."

That's a lie. I noticed all her tattoos the first time I met her and that one has been there for weeks.

We walk to the sandwich shop in silence. I can't think of a single thing to say all of a sudden.

"What do you want to eat?" she asks as we near the restaurant—a little local thing, but not really the trendy variety. The whole place is just mismatched varieties of plastic.

"Not sure yet," I say. "Why don't you order for the guys while I think?"

I read the menu three times, but can't think. Why doesn't she seem to want to be here? And why did she lie to me? And so casually. The only lie—and it wasn't a lie, I remind myself—that Rachel ever told me, was about the cancer. Rather it was her *not* telling me about the cancer right away. The only thing I could change about us—the people we were, the way we handled it—was that. All these years later, I still wish she'd told me. By the time I get to the counter, I still don't know what's on the menu, so I choose the first sandwich. Turkey on rye, even though I'm not a huge fan of turkey and I hate rye.

Nora's chosen a tomato basil chicken on focaccia, and when we get our food a few minutes later, hers looks much better than my sagging sandwich and stinky bread.

"Should we sit?" she says, and I shrug, still thinking about cancer—how it grows, multiplies, takes.

I bite into a chip. "How long do they take to heal?" I ask, pointing to her tattoo. If I came all the way here, I might as well give her the benefit of the doubt.

She sighs. "It's not new. I just...I don't know. I had an awkward moment. And sometimes they do hurt—those spots, especially on the arms."

"Interesting," I say. "I didn't realize tattoos left people with pain."

"They don't usually," she says. "Mine are over scars." She takes a huge bite of her sandwich, fiddles with her napkin, doesn't say more.

Scars? "How's school going?" I ask.

"You're not going to ask me about the scars?" she says.

"Do you want me to?" I say.

"Not yet," she replies.

I poke at my sandwich, eat a tomato off of it. "Okay, then, tell me about school."

"But I will one day," she says. "Tell you about the scars. And school was good. I'm going to take my first engineering class next semester."

"Really?" I ask, genuinely interested. "And what do you start with?"

"Well," she says. "Trigonometry. I, uh, failed it in high school. Actually, I didn't even finish it."

"Trigonometry?" I ask.

"Yeah," she says. "And high school."

For a few minutes, we just chew. I'm not sure what to think. Somehow she's managed to surprise me again. Maybe a few too many surprises. But she is being candid—no lies. She opened up about the tattoo. Fair enough. And the truth is that I like finding out about her. I like the sound of her voice, especially when she talks about the things she's planning to do. I like her smile when she talks about taking trig. I even like the nervous way she fiddles with her napkin and how her voice pitches higher when she tells me something she's worried about saying. But the truth is that she just dropped a couple of huge bombs, and that makes me a little worried too.

"I wasn't going to tell you this," she says. "I'm getting nervous and blurting out weird things."

"No," I say. "It's cool. So you, uh, dropped out."

"Yeah," she says. "Family problems. Big ones. And I just kind of lost myself for a while. And then, well, I came back, got a job, started at the community college. They have an, um, transition program. And if I pass all my classes there, if I get my degree, they won't even care about high school."

"It's true," I say. "I nearly failed trig myself. And no one cares at all now, as long as I can get the code on their computers fixed. No one's ever mentioned a single triangle."

She smiles, popping an olive into her mouth. I notice the lips again, think about touching them, try to bring myself back. She does it for me. "You like your work?" she asks.

"I do," I say, tossing a final chip in my mouth and crinkling up the bag.

"And how long have you been doing it?"

"Almost four years now. Bit of a career shift for me."

"After your divorce?" she asks.

The word hits me like a gray block that I can't interpret. "Divorce?" I ask.

"Yeah," she says slowly, carefully. "Gabby. I just assumed…"

"Oh," I say, cutting her off. "Yeah. I…" I wrap the remains of my food up in a tight ball. "I'm widowed actually."

Her hands have been dancing nervously over everything the whole time. Now they fall to her lap and rest there. "Oh my gosh. I'm such a moron. I'm so sorry. You were just so young and I assumed…"

"Yeah, cancer," I say, and that's all. I don't know what's wrong with me; I'm not mad, but my mouth feels sealed and heavy.

She fidgets with her napkin. "Must be really hard."

"It is."

The guy behind the counter plops a huge bag of

sandwiches down and nods to Nora. She glances at the clock on her phone. "Wow, guess we better go."

I nod.

"Aiden," she says as we're leaving. "Thanks for coming. I'm really glad you did."

"Yeah," I say. It's the word of the day apparently. Am *I* glad I did? I'm not sure.

"I'm sorry if I made it awkward—overshared or something." She's walking quickly, probably worried about getting back to work on time. "I felt like you should know a few things."

"You were fine," I say. "I liked your sharing."

"I'm sorry I asked about your wife."

I don't have an answer to such a straightforward comment. All these years, and I can't respond. My brain is clashing together like it doesn't know words.

She looks down at the bag of sandwiches. I look at her face. She's younger than I am, probably by about five years. That makes her maybe twenty-eight or twenty-nine. Twenty-nine and pulling her life together.

"Well," she says. "I'll see you around."

"Okay," I respond. "I'll be back if anything goes wrong with the car." I feel a bit of a goodbye in my own words, the *I won't call you*. It's not what I was planning to say, or think; it's not why I came. So what's happening?

"I do owe you dessert," she adds with her half smile. It's still charming.

"You don't owe me anything." I look into her eyes, meaning it. I touch the firefly on her shoulder, just for a moment. She doesn't pull back, but my own fingers flit away. "It was nice to talk to you, Nora."

She nods and heads into the shop, her shoulders drooping a little, maybe from the weight of the sandwiches. I slump into my car, look over to the passenger seat and see the chocolate sitting there. Close my eyes. Thrust the car into gear. Push back all the feelings banging around, until they're just a dull throb behind my eyes.

CHAPTER 20

ONE AND A HALF YEARS EARLIER

G abby won an art contest in first grade for a picture she'd drawn of her mother. When I got to the parent night, excited to see her drawing, I was surprised to find a picture of a blond woman, straight hair, tall as the paper could hold. She'd drawn a huge version of a person that looked nothing at all like the vibrant, curvy, brunette woman who had woken up every night for over a year to feed and comfort a troubled, skinny, squalling baby.

I wasn't sure if she'd forgotten what Rachel looked like, despite all the stick figure drawings hung on her wall—she'd been so young—or if this had been her attempt at creating a birth mother.

Either way, I figured it was time for another trip to the beach. I took a few days off work, loaded up the car with a couple of bags. Then, I hauled pictures out of the attic—mostly scrapbooks that Rachel had made. Whole albums of keepsakes and ribbon, pictures cut with specialty scissors and smoothed onto thick, decorative paper. The seven-hour drive. To spend a few days looking at albums, watching home videos. Gabby crawling with Rachel trailing behind. Gabby tottering in those first precious steps into Rachel's open arms. All the laughing. All the clapping. Gabby saying my name over and over. Dadadada. Rachel trying to teach her the trickier 'M' sound. "Mama, baby. Mama." Gabby laughed at all the laughter. Eyes glowing, leaning in with her first steps, first words. She'd kept leaning in when Rachel's hair went away, when the bandages appeared on Rachel's arms, holding in the IVs, when the bed showed up in the living room, when the curves of my wife turned to angles. Still, Gabby sat on her lap. Still, all the pictures were filled with smiles. So many. It seemed almost impossible to count them, those smiles.

I didn't show the funeral pictures. Neither of us was ready. I hadn't even brought them, though I knew just where they were stored, along with a few precious pieces of jewelry Rachel had loved—things I planned to give Gabby one day when she was grown.

"Why?" Gabby asked when the vacation was over and we were driving home. "Why did she get sick?"

"I don't know," I said.

"Will you get sick?" Gabby asked.

The question caught me off guard, and even though I'd sworn to always tell Gabby the truth, I didn't quite this time. "I might get sick," I said, "just normal sick. But I won't die, not till I'm old." It wasn't something a person should ever promise—to not get sick enough to die, but I made the promise anyway, thinking only later about my job as a volunteer firefighter.

I wouldn't have to get sick to die.

CHAPTER 21

PRESENT

I get home from work to find a chocolate cake on my doorstep. A lean tower in a tall white box, like it's been bought, though looking at it, I know it hasn't. The box is generic. No stickers or insignias or branding of any type. No shop sticker to seal it closed. The cake itself is a beautiful three-layer cylinder—all chocolate—but miniature. The cake rounds are about six inches wide instead of the usual size, which makes the cake appear unusually tall, like a skinny brown Dr. Seuss hat. At the top, it's decorated it with bicycles. Bicycles. A large cluster of them made entirely from tempered chocolates of different colors. Brown and white of course, but also red, peach, seafoam green. Each one piled and stacked in different ways against the others. I realize she hasn't just made me a cake, but a sculpture as well.

She's definitely an artist. I admire the handlebars, wheels, spokes, all somehow painstakingly molded from chocolate. But it's also true that she's an engineer. Each round is cut flat so that it stacks perfectly with a quarter inch of frosting between the layers. The outside a precisely edged thing. And the bicycles —a structure that could withstand the packaging and then the travel.

I look up on the thought, toward my door. My address would have been easy enough to get with the billing information and all. But she didn't have a car. She hadn't biked for sixty miles with a cake in the basket—no one was a good enough engineer for that —so how had she gotten here? Bus? Ride with a friend? An Uber? That would have cost her a fortune.

I move the cake to the table, set it there like a centerpiece. I feel like I'll have to leave it there forever. I mean, how could I ever eat such a creation?

I hear Gabby's laugh at the door. Her carpool ride must have arrived and I can hear her giggling with one of the other girls at the door. "Dad," she calls in. "Can Lacie stay and have dinner with us?"

"What does her mom think?" I ask absently, still trying to figure out how Nora made and then stacked the bikes.

"She said it was fine."

"Even though she went to all the trouble to pick you girls up?"

"Yeah," Gabby calls.

"Then it's good with me. I can take Lacie home around seven tonight."

Both girls squeal in the joy of it.

I remember that Lacie's mom is recently divorced, just in time to hear her tap tap at the front door. "Hey Aiden," she says, the clink of her bracelets bouncing around in my empty hallway, her perfume floating all the way to the kitchen. I like Lacie's mom, but she smells like a woman on the rebound prowl, and I don't want to find myself the prey at the end of it.

"Hey Natalie," I say, hurrying out of the kitchen just as she seems to be hurrying in. We almost bump into each other and she scoots around me into the kitchen.

"Okay with you if the girls stay and play?" she asks, her hair in fresh waves.

"Yeah, sure," I say, just as she claps her hands together.

"It's your birthday," she says, looking at the cake and then pulling me in for a hug.

"Oh, no," I mutter, trying to disentangle myself. "Just an, uh…"

Gabby notices the cake and through some type of tiny woman's intuition starts chanting, "Daddy's got a girlfriend. Daddy's got a girlfriend."

Natalie releases me in a rush. "Oh, your girlfriend got you this?" she says, her cheeks flushing.

"An, um, friend," I say.

Natalie smiles. She may be on the prowl, but she's not a jerk. "A friend, huh. On your not-birthday. Just because. That cake."

Gabby continues her chant. "Daddy's got a girl-friend. Daddy's got a girlfriend."

"Well, that's sweet," Natalie says. "Seven o'clock then?"

"Yeah," I say.

"You be good, Miss Lacie. I'll see you in a bit." She swoops down and gives her daughter a lipstick kiss.

"Do we get to eat it, Aiden?" Lacie asks.

"You know, I guess we do," I say. "Let's hope Nora is as good a cook as she is a designer. You girls go play outside and I'll call for a pizza."

More squealing. I'll never stop being amazed at how many high-pitched noises girls can make. I pull out my phone, see Nora's number sitting there right below Neo's Pizza. Pause. My finger over the button. I need to thank her, at the very least. But my finger moves up. I'll thank her soon. For now, one double supreme and one plain cheese. That should have everyone covered.

CHAPTER 22

ELEVEN YEARS EARLIER

I met Rachel in the least romantic place in the universe—reclined on the chair at her dentistry. I'd chipped a tooth the night before (which meant, incidentally, that the first time I saw her, I looked nothing like a dashing movie star firefighter and more like a backwoods country boy with a janky tooth). My buddy had told me that Rachel was the right dentist to fix it. To this day, I don't know if he meant, *Go meet her; she's hot.* Or just, *She does a great job with teeth.* Both were true.

I spent the entire office visit gazing into her hazelnut eyes, the left one spiked with a deep coffee-colored line, a few stray curls bouncing against her temples.

She spent the visit gazing at my teeth, which—fortunately—were clean and decent except for the broken one. Her voice was soft, buttery. I always loved that voice. She cooed her way through the appointment, telling me each thing she was going to do next to fix the tooth. She might as well have been reading poetry.

When she sat me up at the end of the visit, with my numb and drooling mouth, I wanted nothing more than to ask her for her number. I knew that maybe this wasn't quite the best time. I did it anyway, and she looked at me like she was seeing me for the first time—something besides my mouth. "I'm so sorry," she said, pushing back her rolling chair. "I don't date patients."

"Well," I replied. "Then I'll call you when I'm not." Though what I really said, with my numb mouth, was, "Well, sen I'll call syou when I'n not."

She'd smiled, trying to hide it behind her paperwork. But I'd seen it—her own flash of straight, round teeth, though one eye tooth crooked in just a little more than it should have. And I liked that about her—that imperfect tooth in her world of perfect mouths.

I called her the next day. She turned me down again. "You're still in the system," she'd said, laughing.

After that, I called reception and got myself

removed as a patient. "Were you unhappy with your care, Mr. Billings?"

"Not at all," I replied. "Best experience I've had at the dentist in years."

The receptionist had cleared her throat. "And you want to be *removed* as a patient?" she'd replied.

"As quickly as possible," I said.

I remember walking in with Rachel after we were a couple, making eye contact with the receptionist, Macie. I remember her squinting at me like she was trying to place a face, the moment of recognition, the dawning of realization. And then the laugh. I'd liked Macie instantly. Which was good, because she and Rachel were close.

When Macie came to Rachel's funeral, her face was almost as pale as mine, except for the dark gray circles around her eyes. She'd held my hand, held it a long time by the casket, even after others had moved past. Two weeks later, she'd tendered her resignation, gotten a new job at a different clinic, then later —as though dentistry was still too close to Rachel— at the police station.

"It's kind of like you said a few years ago," she said when I called to ask why. "Best experience I've had in years. And now I need to be removed as quickly as possible."

"You remember that?" I asked.

"I'm good at remembering," she said. "Sometimes too good. It just isn't the same without her."

"You have no idea."

We had cried. Both of us. Hard. And it was the best I'd felt in months—a final gift from Rachel, from her office, her work.

Macie still sent Gabby a birthday present every year, and gave me a call on my own birthday.

CHAPTER 23

PRESENT

I send a thank you note to Nora. Just a few lines, ending with, "Gabby loved it too. She said anyone who gave cake like that was a friend worth keeping." It's not exactly what she said —something more along the lines of, "She must really like you, Daddy, to make a cake like this." I left out any mention of the "Daddy's got a girlfriend" chant too.

I don't really expect to hear back from Nora—I left her so abruptly, so rudely, my heart all tied up in knots; and then she did this nice thing. I really do wish I could keep her as a friend. Maybe I wish for more, but I was surprised by how little I could talk about Rachel, how quickly my mouth and brain shut off, how sad it made me to hear the word 'divorce'—

sadder than thinking of her dying, and that just didn't make sense.

Nora shows up at my house two nights later. "Got your note," she says.

"How'd you get here?" I ask. Unintentionally rude. Again.

"I'm sorry. I should have called." She glances back over her shoulder.

"No," I reply, reaching for an arm, holding her wrist. "I didn't mean...I wasn't trying to sound harsh. I'm so sorry. I was honestly just curious."

She looks back at me, the fingers flying over her messenger bag, nervous. "I have a friend whose mom lives up here. One of the guys from work, actually. He said he could bring me."

"That's nice of him."

"Do you want to go for a walk?" she asks.

Gabby is at Lacie's house for a post-carpool play date. "Sure," I say, grabbing my keys and locking the door.

"Is this really too much?" she says, gesturing with her hands toward the street, my house. "My showing up."

The truth is that it's pretty normal, except we don't live in the same city and she doesn't have a car, which makes it feel like a lot of effort, which makes it feel...I don't know... more intense. "No," I say.

"That sounded like a question," she replies, as we make our way down the street. I notice that she's wearing joggers, a t-shirt, and tennis shoes. Like she intended to move while she talked. I'm still in khakis and my loafers.

"No," I say again, trying to make it more convincing—to her, to me. Then, for reasons I could never fathom, I ask, "Why don't you have a car?"

We're walking past a park, practically jogging with how fast she's moving. She takes a sharp left and we veer onto a path. It's cloudy, almost misty outside and not too many people are out. Before answering, she speed walks her way into a part of the path where trees hang low and dark over our heads, where it's harder to see her face. "Because I don't have a license."

There's more to the answer, and I slow down under the trees, waiting for it.

"Because?"

"Because I never have. I left home at seventeen, hitchhiked across the state, got a job at a bar."

"But you were too—"

"—young." She finishes for me. "I know. I lied about my age. I lied about a lot of things back then."

I swallow. Between the clouds, the setting sun, and the overhanging trees, it suddenly feels like night. "Why?" I ask. It's a jerk question. I don't even really want the answer, because I know it can't possibly be good.

"Because my father abused me, had for years. He broke my jaw." She traces a line along her face that I've never noticed before. Sure enough, it looks like an incision made for a surgery, an incision she must have covered with make-up on most days.

"At the hospital my dad told them I'd gotten drunk and fallen in the shower. He couldn't even just say I'd fallen; he had to add the drunk part. It wasn't true," she says. "When I was finished at the hospital, well, there was this nurse and she...she knew. She didn't say anything, didn't ask for my story. But she could tell. After I'd healed, the doctor signed me out and they were going to call my dad, but this nurse, she slipped me three hundred-dollar bills and a bus pass, told me I needed to get out. Then she wheeled me to the bus stop at the front of the hospital. By the time my dad got there, I was gone."

I move my mouth, but no words come out.

"Do you know I can't remember her name? I was on pain meds and things were all foggy. I could never contact her, never thank her. I don't even know what they told my dad, or if she lost her job. I just rode that bus for six hours, nothing more than a bottle of Tylenol and those hundred dollar bills in my pocket. I needed a job where I could make money, good money; and a diner somewhere wasn't going to cut it."

"Why are you telling me this?" I ask.

"Because I want you to know." It's all she says. But there's more. I feel it under her words. *I want you to know before we dance around sending notes, giving gifts, bouncing back and forth, maybe trying this out. I want you to know before you reject me. I want you to know all the reasons you should. So that it doesn't hurt when you do.* All of that bubbling under her sentences that run together in a rush.

I can't fully process it, can only think as her story rolls out, *Do I want to know?* But before I can even process that, my mouth seems to open itself and ask, "And then?"

"But a bar wasn't really a good idea. As anyone who isn't a seventeen-year-old runaway could probably tell you. Men came every night. Sometimes they were good looking, sometimes they left good tips, sometimes they had grabby hands. Often they bought me drinks."

"And you drank those drinks?"

"Yeah," she says, looking at me with her green eyes under those black-shadowed trees. "It wasn't the right choice, but everything hurt—hurt in a way that even a generous nurse couldn't fix with as much money as she could spare. Can you understand that, Aiden? Understand how everything could hurt so much?"

I shake my head 'no.' I can sort of imagine it—it hurt when Rachel died, so much. But not in this way Nora is describing. Rachel's death hurt for the sweetness of our life. Nora's hurt though—it was an acidic thing, burning on top, then burning its way down in layers, never knowing when, if, it would stop. Something I haven't had to understand in my life.

"That's an honest answer," she says, reaching out and touching my wrist. She leaves her fingers there, and I feel the warmth, the fire even, of her fingertips. I notice her curves in the shadows, the way the outfit hugs her. My throat feels thick.

"There was one guy. Maybe twenty-five. I don't know. He worked at the Toyota factory and always came in Friday with a wad of cash. He liked me. And I liked him. He had brown eyes, curly wild hair, sharp features, even good teeth." She laughs a hard laugh, touching the line of scar along her jaw. "He always bought me drinks, even took me to a movie a couple times. That was high courtship in my mind. And then one weekend he came, said he had to move, wanted me to come. Do you know I didn't even ask why?"

"You were seventeen."

"I was worse than seventeen," she says. "I guarantee that at seventeen Gabby will know to ask why."

I realize she's no longer holding my wrist, that my fingers have slipped down and are wrapping through hers. She nearly pulls back; I can feel it. And then she doesn't.

"I found out the reason later—why he had to move. He lost his job. Lost his job because during a routine check, some dogs found meth in his locker. I didn't know that, but do you know what?"

"It wouldn't have mattered if you did."

She almost cries then. I see the tears spring into her eyes, the way they get red around the rims, and that red makes the green so much brighter.

"I was ready to leave that bar anyway, those grabby men. I was ready for a change. But this was the wrong change. We moved close to here, to this city."

I raise my eyebrows, a little surprised at that detail. "You got a job with Joe?" I ask.

"Not even close," she replies. "I didn't get a job at all. Neither did he. Which makes you wonder how we lived. He bought a little trailer on the outskirts of town. He had some money saved from his job. After that ran out, we lived by lying. We lived by stealing. We lived a meth life of meth people." She breaks from my hand and holds out her arms. "I told you they were scarred."

"Oh no," I say, letting my own arms hang limp.

"It's not something I'm proud of. Nothing I did in those years is something I'm proud of. It just is."

"And how did you get out? Why did you get out, if you were caught up in that life?"

"Do you know that meth makes people paranoid sometimes? They'll be coming down off of a high and suddenly think that everyone is out to get them."

I nod. I had been a firefighter after all. My work had led me to addicts and their sometimes burning houses on a regular enough basis. They were horrible patients most of the time—mean, empty. The memory of it makes me step away from her. Those were not good calls.

"He was coming down one night, started screaming at me, pulling my hair, calling me names —terrible names. I'd been called those names before, by my dad. They might not have been enough to shake me up. But he had this old gun in a case. He took it out, started waving it around, said he was going to kill me dead—a lying, cheating girl like me. Then he loaded it up, held it to my neck. I don't know how long. It felt like nothing and forever all at once. Maybe it was."

She stops in her story, sits down on a bench, like she's done, like the memory has worn her out and she won't go on. I sit beside her. I can't figure out if I want to wrap her up in a hug or get up and run away. I settle for something middle-of-the road and sit, stiff and straight, against the bench. The birds are settling in for the night and every once in a while something that looks like a bat, but might be a swallow, swoops into one of the trees.

"I didn't talk as he held that gun against me; it wouldn't have helped, but after who-knows-how long, he took the gun off my neck, started pacing around, swearing, throwing stuff. And then—like addicts do after a high—he fell into a deep, long sleep." She doesn't look at me, just keeps talking. "I still had a hundred dollar bill. I'd saved one from the nurse, hadn't needed it. I took the earliest bus I could and checked myself into a mental institution."

"And him?"

"He shot himself the night after I left."

I lean over, put my head in my hands. I look like I'm grieving, but I'm trying to remember the call. I would have been working then. It would have come out from dispatch. Police and EMS would have taken it, but we might have gone too if they needed support. Gunshot wound, probably to the head, self-inflicted. But I can't remember it, or even hearing about it. There are too many like it, some meth head with a gun in a trailer. It's a story on repeat.

Not like Nora's story at all. She isn't dead in a trailer with enough drug in her veins to wreck a train. She is here now with clear skin and lovely eyes and red hair and white teeth. White teeth. So square, so perfect. Not like Rachel's crooked eyetooth at all.

"Did your dad knock out your teeth?" I ask. "Or that boyfriend?"

The question surprises her, me too. "I'm sorry," I say quickly. "I don't know why I said that. It was rude."

She shrugs. "Neither. The drugs ruined them, and then, when I had enough money, I paid to have them fixed and replaced." She closes her mouth, smiles with her lips sealed.

"My wife was a dentist," I say. "I always notice teeth."

She nods, and I know I've made her insecure. And then she presses her lips together like she's made a decision, stands. "Thanks, Aiden, for listening. I just wanted you to know." She pulls her phone out of her pocket, sends a text; I'm guessing to her friend.

"You're not going to tell me about your recovery."

She smiles. It's still crooked and I still like it, but one side is almost drooping into a frown. "I can tell that you don't really want to hear it."

"Why do you say that?"

"Because it's true."

Is it true? Why wouldn't I want to know about her recovery? Why did I let her tell me all the ugly parts of her story and not the beautiful ones?

"Of course I want to know," I insist, but then my own phone buzzes. "Oh shoot," I say. "Gabby's friend's mom is dropping her off. I've got to get back." I reach out, squeeze her hand. She squeezes back, but it's just to be polite, that squeeze.

I take a few steps away, then turn back. "My wife got cancer in her uterus. She had it way before either of us knew it. She found out before I did. And she didn't tell me, and it's one of the great sadnesses of my life—that she didn't tell me. Thank you for your story."

It's a big story, a story for a woman I doubt I can date. Still, I'm thankful to have heard it. She seems thankful to have said it, to have gotten something out into the air. But she's sad too, sad that I don't want to know the rest. Maybe I'm sad about it as well, but I'm getting another text from Natalie and don't have time to think about it.

We hurry back to the main road, both of us silent. A car rounds the corner, slowing to pick her up.

"Take care of yourself," I say.

"I will," she replies. And I can tell it's true—a promise she made to herself, part of the recovery I'm afraid to find out about.

G abby's waiting on the porch when I get home, arranging leaves on the steps with Lacie.

"So sorry. I went for a walk and lost track of time," I say to Natalie through the window of her car.

"No worries," she replies, waving Lacie over to the car. "Did you have fun?"

"Fun?" I ask.

"On your date?"

"Oh, I wasn't on a date. Just a walk." She looks at my clothes, my loafers, and shrugs. "You're driving the girls tomorrow, right?"

"Right," I say absently as Gabby and Lacie tear themselves away from each other in the way of second grade girls.

I fumble with my keys in the darkness and Gabby asks me the same question. "Did Nora come? Did you have fun?"

"How do you know she came?" I ask.

"You never go for walks," she says.

"We just talked," I say.

"About what?"

"Oh, life."

"Did you get her cake recipe?" Gabby asks. "Me and Lacie want to try it and take it to Miss Farr for the Halloween party."

I shake my head. "Oh, honey, that's sweet, but it's not a very easy cake to make. Maybe we can just buy something."

"Buying it's not very special," she says with a pout, her green globes of eyes swimming in that small face.

I rub my neck, trying to work out a knot I didn't notice earlier. "Well, we can do something else."

"Oh, Daddy," she says suddenly. "Did you break up?" She hugs my waist and I lean down and lift her up. She's getting heavy, the gangly legs always dangling.

"Oh Gabsy," I say. "We didn't break up. We couldn't. We were just friends."

"Breaking up with friends is even sadder," she replies, wrapping her arms around my neck and squeezing like crazy. I squeeze back, realizing with an ache in my throat that she's right.

INTERLUDE

NORA

The thing about deciding to get clean... Well, it isn't just a day or moment. It isn't just one choice, but many. Even when people talk about their rock-bottom moment, sure, that's a thing. But there are plenty of other moments, and they matter too.

Me? I suppose I had dozens. One—the night I came home from the hospital after being clean for months. One—the night Clive almost killed me. Gun to my head, bits of my hair torn out, all the accusations just like my daddy those years ago. One—my first night in that state-run mental institution—inmates screaming like we'd signed up for layers of hell, not medical assistance for our addictions.

Then three days later when they let me out, when I still didn't know what to do. So I did what addicts usually do. I went back home. Living with Clive was better than sleeping on the street, right? Not true, but I wasn't in a place to know that then. The bus rolled up after ten at night and I walked the mile out to the trailer park. I remember looking at it, realizing that once it had been yellow, but I'd never thought of it as that color, never realized it had color at all.

Only the screen door was closed, which I assumed meant that Clive was either on a high high and not caring, or down low and fast asleep. At the places in between, he usually locked the door.

Turned out the screen was locked, but since it had a huge hole in the side, that didn't much matter. I reached my hand through the hole, turned the lock, and then paused before letting myself in. I'd done so many hard things in my life and kept coming back to this. This. A once-yellow trailer with a busted screen door, a placed that housed a man I'd just run from and come back to. Like it was the best I could get. Maybe it was. I slumped my shoulders and walked in. The place stunk like the garbage hadn't been taken out for days, like a rat had died in one of those glue traps Clive set out. Great. All the lights were out except a little one over the stove. Probably meant he was asleep somewhere. Yup. Sprawled along the kitchen floor, one arm out at an awkward angle. Passed out hard. Nothing strange at this point in my life about the man I lived with being out cold on the kitchen floor; most normal thing in the world. Even that arm bent up the wrong way, elbow sticking out awkwardly—all I could think was, "Looks like he's gone and broken his arm. Now I'm gonna have to take him to the ER when he sobers up."

It ticked me off, so without further examination, I walked up to him and gave him a hard nudge with my foot, the kind of nudge that says, "Wake up, you idiot." And the strangest thing happened—a little swirl of flies shot up into the air.

I still didn't get it.

I looked down at my shoes and there, on the floor, was a little puddle of brownish liquid—dried and disgusting. At that point, things started slowing down in my brain. I looked at that dirty spot for what felt like an hour, though it couldn't have been more than a minute, and what did I come up with? Well, I honestly hoped it was blood. If he'd gone and crapped himself, I'd make him take himself to the ER.

And even though blood might seem like a really bad thing to a normal person, I wasn't a normal person. I figured Clive has gone and busted his head when he fell, or that he'd knocked it into something when he was high. Wasn't like it hadn't happened before.

I knelt to flip him over, wake him up—the moron.

I put my fingers to his shoulders and my brain, still sluggishly trying to gather the pieces—this behind-the-times brain of mine, it somehow managed to notice that the shoulder I grabbed was cold. Not chilly trailer floor cool, but cold like I hadn't felt before in a shoulder.

My hands hadn't caught up to this realization yet, however. By the time my brain informed me of this unnaturally cold skin, I'd lifted a shoulder off the dirty vinyl floor.

And now my brain had another problem because there, beneath him, lay a brown-black sticky mass wriggling with little white larval bodies.

I let go of the shoulder, a soft thud back to the floor. My gaze—slow as molasses in January—took in his white cheek, the sticky stuff, the smell of the trailer. A smell I'd assumed was just old food. Now I watched his back, the way it stayed still instead of rising and falling. Stiff, heaven help me, he was stiff.

At about this time, my brain caught up and I skittered backwards, letting out a curse or a wail or some animal combination of the two.

And you know, for a moment I didn't call 911. For a second I sat there thinking I couldn't call because they'd assume I killed him, that I'd go to prison for the rest of my life. For a moment, I almost ran. Again.

And then, some piece of sanity or humanity or soberness or intelligence beat its way through my thick skull.

With shaking hands, I stumbled over to his phone on the counter. Battery at five percent. He never let me have one. Told me the landline was good enough for me. Of course we didn't have one of those either—not really—because he hadn't paid the bill in over four months.

I swiped up, hammered out 911. It legitimately took me three tries to hit the numbers right, and I was down to four percent battery life.

When the woman picked up, she was all business, asking for details like address that my brain had temporarily stored in a file I couldn't access.

"The trailer park," I said. "Off Highway 92. A brownish trailer."

"Do you have the address, ma'am?"

"Country Estates Trailer Park," I stammered out, like I'd accomplished some feat of genius in remembering.

"Do you have the house number?" she asked, all cool to my burning heat.

I had to stand up, look outside.

"Twenty-five," I said.

"I'm sending out a unit. Is the patient unresponsive?" she asked.

I looked at his dead body. "Yes."

"Do you know how long?" she asked.

I shook my head, realized she couldn't see it, mumbled, "No."

Then, in a corner of the trailer, I saw it, the dark silhouette of the gun he must have dropped as he fell.

"Oh help," I whispered.

"They'll be there as fast as possible," she said, her tone soothing, but still business. A voice that had said those words so many times, she no longer heard them.

And then my brain, that traitor, it remembered the name of my street. "Hollyhock," I blurted.

"Excuse me?" she replied.

"The name of my street. 25 Hollyhock."

"They're en route," she said.

"He's dead," I said, because what else was there?

"The ambulance is five minutes away," she replied. Because what else was there?

The coroner arrived forty-five minutes after the medics pronounced Clive solidly, decayingly dead. Somehow, even though I had literal crusty blood on my hands from touching him, I was not convicted of murder. Apparently, even without a suicide note, the scene was pretty cut and dried. It took the detective, a woman, all of ten minutes to finish up on scene. "You found him today?" she asked.

I nodded, not offering any more information.

Strangely, she didn't ask me more. Not, "Who are you to him? Where have you been for the last three days? Why do you think he did this?" Definitely not, "How could you let this happen?" Instead, when she was done, she patted me on the shoulder. There was something in that pat, something that said, *Glad you weren't home, hon.*

The body was gone; the weapon was gone; the smell was not really gone—would it ever be completely gone—but the coroner had even cleaned up the mess underneath Clive.

And the thing is, I could have stayed. I'd lived here for the last five years. But when I looked around, I realized that the trailer wasn't mine. The car wasn't mine. I didn't even know how to drive it. None of the bills were mine. I'd come back to a life that wasn't mine, that shouldn't be mine.

I had forty dollars left of my last hundred dollar bill. Two wadded up twenties in my pocket. In addition to that, I found an ounce of pot stashed in an old sock. Not exactly mine, but no longer his, I guess. Somehow the rest of the drugs were gone.

Whether he'd used them, burned them, sold them, or hid them, I'd never know.

One backpack with a pair of old jeans, a couple t-shirts, none of them clean. I didn't have a wallet, so I shoved my money in a different sock. On the way out, I sold the marijuana sock to my neighbor for ten bucks. That would be Denny's for dinner.

Something had broken. And something had fixed. It took me a few more months to untangle which was which.

I wouldn't be completely sober for six more months.

I wouldn't be employed for another month after that.

Wouldn't have a house (or a room in one) till just after Christmas, when a spot in the state-run recovery program opened up.

After that I upgraded to an apartment with a roommate, got a job at Joe's. By then I had clean hair, clean clothes, shoes that fit. I spent my first five months' income fixing my teeth and covering my scars with tattoos. Beautiful things. A new me for a new life.

CHAPTER 24

NINE YEARS EARLIER

achel hadn't called me when she had her first miscarriage. Just a text. "I think I'm losing the baby."

By the time I got home from work, the toilet was filled with blood, a small blot of dead fetus floating in a sealed Tupperware container. "Doctor told me to bring it in when we went to the hospital." Her words were dull, flat. Like she was a nurse at the ER, distanced from all this stuff that was going on around her.

I took her hand. "Are you okay?"

"It won't stop," she said. "I just keep bleeding."

It was true. She loaded up with pads and bled through them every ten minutes. "Guess I need a diaper," she said as we pulled up to the ER. It was meant to be funny, but neither of us laughed. The dead baby sloshed around in the Tupperware on her lap and when she stood up, the stack of Chux pads I'd put on the seat was also splotched with blood.

You wonder sometimes how women died so often before the advent of modern medicine. And then your wife has a miscarriage and in half an hour loses so much blood that it seems impossible that she has any left. By the time we walked into the ER, her face had paled to a dusty white. They wheeled her to a room, helped her gown up.

She passed the rest of the placenta within minutes and I could see the relief on everyone's faces —doctor, nurse, Rachel. I could feel it on my own as well.

Even so, the drive home felt so much worse. Going to the hospital, we had had a purpose, a need. The slow slog home felt like all of that had washed away. Instead of a fetus, she was carrying a bottle of water to rehydrate. That was it, not even a pill, like nothing had happened.

I cleaned the bathroom, did a load of laundry. She lay down.

"I'm really sorry," I told her as we got into bed, two tired bodies on cold, clean sheets.

"It was your baby too," she said, with a bit of a dagger in her voice.

"I'm sad, too," I said. A truth that wasn't enough for that night.

"Then where are your tears?" She turned from me and I from her. I had plenty of tears, pent up and burning at my eyes.

The next week, she apologized. "The doctor warned me my hormones would go haywire," she said. "Not that I'm trying to make excuses. I wasn't very nice for a few days."

I wouldn't have called her mean. Harsh, angry, lost. And definitely hormonal, though you couldn't have paid me to use that word at the time.

"You were fine," I said. I meant it too.

She spent the next three months recovering, started on a prenatal vitamin, ate like a saint.

Six months after the first baby, we lost another. Almost to the day. She didn't get angry that time, just quiet. And five months after that, when the third died, she simply said, "I'm done."

"I'm so sorry."

What else was there to say? It took several more months before she even considered drugs. All the moods, the weight gain, the acne, the everything horrible that a woman spends her life avoiding. That's what she spent a year suffering through. In vitro came up at the end of the year and she just held up her hands, didn't even answer the doctor when he said the words. Stood up, walked out of the room. "I guess that's a 'no,'" he said, surprisingly cheerful.

"Yeah, I think so," I said. Then, because I wanted a baby too and was lost too, I asked, "Should I try to convince her?"

"I wouldn't recommend it," he said. "She'll come around if she wants and if she doesn't, bringing it up won't help a thing." He did slide a small brochure to me, one about an adoption agency. "An agency that I recommend. If it ever comes to that. Don't open it up over dinner tonight—for all that's sacred in your life. Don't open it for at least three months. But then maybe have a look. The world has options, even though right now if feels like every door has slammed closed."

I didn't look in three months, or in four either. A few months later I found it while cleaning out my desk, sat on the bed, read every word. Another week passed before Rachel saw it, and asked about it. We opened it together, saw all the precious faces staring back at us. Something about it was the right moment. Enough time for her not to think how unfair it was—these unwanted children when we'd wanted so hard. If there's ever really enough time. But there's only so long you can look at the face of a baby and resent that it wasn't yours. Especially if it could be. We filled out the papers.

She started humming again. I hadn't noticed that she had stopped, not until it came back. The sweet sound of her voice when she got home from work. We hugged more, sat closer together. But no one child sang to our hearts. Not until that day at the station when the woman in a ball cap walked in and handed me a baby with a bruise lining her forehead.

Just a few weeks later, we were fostering her. And a few months after that, she was ours. Ours. The most precious word in all the world.

And then Rachel had to go and die.

CHAPTER 25

PRESENT

I ask Natalie out. She turns me down.

"Wouldn't want a guy on the rebound," she says with a devilish smile.

"She was just a friend," I stammer.

"Right, right. But seriously, it might make things weird between us, our girls."

She's not wrong.

I ask out a girl from work instead. She's nice, about my age. Barely over five feet with blue pixied hair. Small, straight teeth with a thin gap between the upper top ones. We nerd over Star Wars and chat about clients and joke all through dinner. It's a lot of fun and I think that I should probably want to ask her out again, but somehow I don't. She gives me a hug at good-bye and high fives me when I see her in the office. Later I hear that she's started dating one of the other women at work. Which knocks out a good two-thirds of my work dating pool, leaving only our sixty-year-old supervisor. I take a pass on that one, happy to have her show me pictures of her new grandbaby instead.

A call comes out for a shed fire. I almost click that I'm coming, then stop myself. I buy a gym membership instead, take Gabby swimming at the pool, and go twice a week to the weight room. It's not a bad choice. I feel better. I look better.

Gabby and I make our own homemade volcano— baking soda and vinegar foaming out of the top—but when she starts looking at YouTube videos for bicycle cakes, I tell her we really should just buy one.

"Okay, Daddy."

Though when I look at her search history, it's clear that she's still scouring her way through cake after cake. I give in, buy a mix, suggest something Halloween themed instead of bicycle themed. She throws her arms around my neck and we spend the next day measuring spheres to create a jack-o-lantern cake. I freeze the layers, just like the Internet says, mix two frostings into orange and black with special frosting gel that it took me nearly fifteen minutes to find at the grocery store. When the layers are hard, we stack and frost them, slather on a thin layer YouTube calls a crumb coat, throw that in the fridge and then begin decorating in earnest.

Earnest is basically how the finished product looks. Somewhat yellow-orange with a little ooze on one side, one black triangle eye and another that is drooping. Gabby tells me it's okay because it's a Halloween cake so it's supposed to be scary. But I can see the disappointment in her eyes. We definitely could have used an engineer on this one.

Moxie comes in, sniffing around, finds a spoon with a bit of leftover cream, and licks it clean.

"Should we scrap it and frost it again?" I ask.

Gabby tilts her head to look at it sideways. "I have an idea," she says. "This is how the cake lady on YouTube does it sometimes." She takes a long, flat knife and without removing any of the black frosting, she smears it. I open my mouth to stop her, but then realize it's kind of swirling with the orange in lines. When she's done, it isn't a jack-o-lantern, but a more abstract and completely beautiful rendering of a pumpkin.

"I love it," I say.

"It's not bad," she replies, testing out her best grown up voice and holding a hand to her chin like she's doing an inspection.

CHAPTER 26

EIGHT YEARS EARLIER

J had wanted Rachel to do in vitro. This was before I remembered the adoption brochure, before Gabby was even on our horizon. I'd wanted a baby. With our little hands, and our little ears, pieces of our brains, pieces of our hearts. Ironically, I hadn't pushed Rachel for a baby earlier in our marriage. I'd been happy with just the two of us. But something about that anticipation—the pregnancy tests and check-ups. It drove me into a sense of longing, of hope. When in vitro felt like our final option —and when it really was our final option for a biological baby—I wanted Rachel to do it.

I didn't say this. Didn't try to push it—just like the doctor had recommended. I just happened to mention babies a lot—how Todd and Kate were going to be churning out another one, the guy from work who'd just had twins. Oh, and that other couple at the other station, they'd been struggling too, but had just gotten a positive pregnancy test.

Can you imagine? Me doing this to my wife? My wife who had spent a year sick on fertility drugs.

I didn't mean to. I'm not even sure at the time I was conscious of it, though I must have known on some level. Must have chosen to ignore certain looks, pretended not to understand the sighs or the nights she went to bed early.

One night, after dinner, Rachel stood up without finishing her food, walked out of the room. I stood too. "What?" I said, throwing my hands up—like the most innocent guy you'd ever met.

"If you don't know..." she growled from the other room.

"Know what?" I followed her. At least I had the sense to do that.

"If you don't know, I'm not sure how much good it will do to tell you," she finished, going into the bathroom and locking the door.

"Rach," I said tapping on it. "Rachel. Just talk to me."

"I'm tired," she said, not opening the door. "I'm tired of talking about babies, thinking about babies, *hearing* about babies. Look, I'm glad for Todd and Kate, for all those other people. If that's what you want me to be, then fine, I'm happy for them. But that's not what you want."

Now I knew she was being unfair. Could I not mention my sister getting pregnant without my wife going nuts? "Come on, Rachel," I said. "That's not fair."

She didn't respond, didn't unlock the door.

"You know I can open this lock with a butter knife," I said.

Still no answer.

I went to the kitchen to get a knife. I was on a roll with the wrong choices.

She walked through the front hall with her keys in hand.

"Where are you going?" I asked.

"I'm tired," she said. "TIRED."

"We're both tired," I said. "This has been really hard."

"You want me to do in vitro," she said, standing in front of the door.

"How is me telling you my sister is pregnant the same as asking you to do in vitro?"

"Your sister," she said, "those twins, a couple from work, tons of random people you keep mentioning."

"Like who?"

"Our neighbor two doors down, your old chief who just had his first grandbaby, the guy at the barbershop who sat next to you, the checker at Walmart. You've mentioned seventeen different babies in the last week."

"You've been counting? Rach, that's on you."

She turned to the door and walked out.

She'd never done that before. We'd had plenty of arguments, quiet nights, empty beds. She'd never left the house like that. In fact, we'd agreed early on in our marriage never to do that—to leave when we were trying to work something out.

She told me later that it didn't feel very much like we'd been trying to work anything out, that she'd needed space, air to breathe.

But that night—that night she came home just before bed, got into her pajamas, and made her way to the guest room.

I went for a run. Didn't matter that it was after nine o'clock. Two could play at this game. I ran past an old lady letting her dog poop on the curb, a couple of teens kissing in a car, a screaming match in the apartment down the street. I ran past a parked stroller, sitting outside the garage like it'd been forgotten. Then I turned around and ran back to it, paused for a moment at the driveway before I walked up to the forgotten stroller, looked at it, touched the handles and felt the firm, cushy plastic against my palms. I pushed at it, only to realize it was locked. I clicked it with my foot, released the wheels. No security systems on these things. I could walk away with it, into the night like I was just a dad with a baby who wouldn't sleep. I moved the stroller, let the wheels spin. I didn't think about security cameras, didn't consider that a theft could ruin my career. I had it halfway down the driveway before I started to cry. Big, ugly man-tears.

I pushed the stroller back up the driveway, next to the garage, so no one would accidentally run over it with their car in the morning. Still crying, I started to jog again, shifting in to a full-on run and then a desperate sprint. As though I could outrun it, these feelings, this missing-ness.

I got home just past midnight, covered in sweat with my left calf threatening to cramp. I tapped on the guest bedroom door. She didn't answer, but I heard her sigh.

"You up?" I asked.

"Of course, I'm up," she snapped.

I opened the door. Not locked. "You were right," I said. "I wanted to try in vitro."

She looked away. I could see it even in the dark.

I stopped, started again. "I wanted *you* to try in vitro."

All the fight left her shoulders. "Why'd you have

to keep doing that?" she asked. "Talking about all those babies."

"I don't know. I didn't really realize I was doing it. But I might have been trying not to realize I was doing it. I don't know. It's all knotted up."

She patted the bed beside her, then caught a whiff of me. "Whoa."

"I almost stole a stroller tonight. That's what it took to realize I'd gone off the deep end a bit."

"A bit."

"Aren't infertile people supposed to go off the deep end? I thought it's what we were known for."

"*You're* not the infertile one," she said. "That's partly what makes it suck so bad."

"*We,*" I said, "are a couple. An infertile one. I'm part of it, part of you."

She rocked against me and I wrapped my disgustingly sweaty arms around her.

"You're gross, man," she said, not moving to leave my arms.

"I know," I said. "You don't need to do in vitro. We're perfect, just the two of us."

"You almost stole a stroller tonight," she said, then tipped her head against my chest, so that the next sentence came out muffled. "Maybe I should at least try it. In vitro, not theft."

"Or maybe you shouldn't," I said. "You've been through a miserable year."

"I have," she said. "My appetite is just barely normalizing after the drugs they gave me. "But time's a wastin'. Maybe I'll call the doctor tomorrow."

I pulled her in tight. "You can, if that's what you really want to do," I said. "But you don't. I don't think so anyway. Listen, you suffered for a year. Why don't you give it another year before you even think about in vitro—or whatever timeframe you want. But some time. Don't even worry about it. I won't mention babies, except Kate's, because I'll have to. And I won't steal any strollers, so you can rest your mind about that."

"What about diapers?" she asked. "Binkies."

"Nothing," I said. "I solemnly swear not to steal any baby-related items, or any other items for that matter. At least in the next year."

She giggled, just a bit, and I rubbed her back, trying to work out some of the lumps from a tense day.

"But don't leave me, Rach. Don't walk out."

"I won't," she said. "I'm sorry I did today. I just… couldn't breathe."

"Because I'd suffocated you?" I asked.

"I wouldn't have said it like that," she said.

I tickled her back.

"Okay, maybe I would have said it like that. Anyway, I'm sorry."

"Me too," I said, kissing her forehead. "Now I'm going to go get a shower. I might be naked when I come back."

"I wouldn't complain about that," she said.

*a*nd I'd like to say that that magical night created a gorgeous magical baby. Just like that. But it didn't. Instead, several other nights and days stacked together to create their own special brand of magic—the afternoon I found the brochure, the first time we looked at the adoption website together, the morning I noticed the completed forms —Rachel's swooping, careful print filling up the boxes. And that final night—the night another woman brought me the baby that would become ours. Ours. Just like I'd always imagined. Not the same body. Not the same mind. But somehow still the same heart.

CHAPTER 27

The day before Gabby's school Halloween party, my car won't start. It'd be easy to tow it to the place down the street, but I don't. I pay the extra hundred bucks to have it taken to Joe's. "A hundred even," the tow guy tells me, "if you pay with cash, not a card." But I don't have a hundred bucks in cash. I think about that sum—what it can buy. A bus ticket. Maybe a week of food. Maybe a fake ID. Maybe a promise for a life you don't have. For me, today, it buys (plus the three percent processing fee) a long tow to a city an hour away. Joe's is cheap, I tell myself. I'll make the money back. It's not a lie.

Nora's not at the desk when I get there. Joe walks in, wiping his hands. "You sabotaging that thing?" he asks.

"Not trying to," I answer.

He grunts. "Nora took the day off. Studying for some test she's nervous about."

"Oh," I say as nonchalantly as I can.

"Took a couple days off a few weeks ago too," he adds, taking my keys and looking me in the eye. "Moped around for a bit."

I have no words.

"She don't mope long, though, that girl. Got to get on with her life."

"Of course," I mumble.

"I'm guessing it's your alternator. Shouldn't cost much or take long neither. We'll have you out of here by eleven."

It feels like a final-ish sort of time.

He's done five minutes before that, hands me my keys.

I've got the day wide open and when I get into my car, I see that they've moved a few things out of the glove compartment. A chocolate bar is one of them.

I get to Nora's apartment, as fidgety as I was the first time I arrived. Maybe worse. I tap on the apartment door, hear a lot of fumbling, some laughter. I take a step back, about to leave, just as the door opens and an unfamiliar woman stares at me. Wide pupils, workout shirt slouching down over one shoulder, hands shaking. "Hey," she says.

"Hi," I say. "You must be Nora's roommate. Is she here?" Something crashes in another room. It sounds like a large piece of glass breaking and I wince, but the crash is followed by more laughter. Male voices.

"Nah, baby," the woman says. "But you wanna come in?"

"No, I…" I stammer. And then I notice her arm, the slight prick of blood at the crook of her elbow. I stare a beat too long.

"Nora will be back tonight," the girl says, closing the door. Her hands shake in a quivering beat along the edge of it as she begins to close it.

"You—" I begin, not knowing how to end.

"Maybe six or seven. She usually comes home to eat something." The girl snorts, like eating is an excess she doesn't understand.

"So, you," I say. "Nora. She—"

"What about her?" the girl asks, edging the door closed, the shudder of her hands still tapping out its unsteady rhythm.

The chocolate bar hangs in my hand. It feels like a poisonous snake I picked up. I hold it by the plastic edge, barely touching it. I haven't seen someone so high for a long, long time. Did Nora introduce her to it, I wonder. Is she really not clean at all? Was that whole thing she told me just a story, a fairytale? Though she wasn't there at the apartment right now, I remind myself. She could be completely ignorant about this whole thing. I think of the shattering glass, the voices of multiple men. It's no good. "Nothing," I say to her roommate, tossing the chocolate into the trash can as I pass. I don't even want to eat it, and I definitely don't want to give it to Gabby.

CHAPTER 28

SEVEN YEARS EARLIER

We'd turned in the initial fostering paperwork a week before Gabby tore into our lives. She wasn't Gabby then. No name. No identity. No strings. That's how it worked with surrenders. A woman could drop off a baby and walk out. We didn't ask questions, take ID, nothing. A final desperate moment for a desperate woman. It was a fantastic program. In my entire career, we'd gotten seven surrenders. Each time, the baby was adopted within six months, and often fostered by the same family before that. A relatively short period of time because it needed no negotiation. No mother who could change her mind—it had already been made up. No family that would interfere. No deciding whether something would be an open or closed adoption, and no worrying about what an open adoption would mean. A physical at the hospital, plenty of paperwork at the adoption agency. Six months to make sure no family members stepped forward. And then done.

As the firefighter who took her in, I had an additional edge. Not any big power, just a little foot in the door. Emergency workers who help with the surrender get priority, much like a family member would, in the adoption process. With most of the paperwork already done, things went fast. Serendipity—that's what Rachel called it. We were a golden couple just sitting right there. They approved us shortly after the surrender.

Jessie didn't even roll her eyes when I told her. I could tell she wanted to, could see the look on her face that she got when we went back to repeat patients, old ladies who had fallen going to the bathroom, or accidentally clicked their Life Alert buttons. A look that wanted to warn or lecture, but didn't.

Kate was not much better. "Aren't you worried, Aiden? This is a troubled child from a very troubled mother. There will be health problems, maybe emotional issues, possibly even some severe disabilities." But I saw the bright green eyes in my mind. So wide and clear. She'd come to us with that bruise, but the baby didn't seem to have been abused.

They'd checked her brain at the hospital, done a thorough physical. Even her weight was good. She cried a lot, and loudly, but so—my mother told me on a rare Sunday phone call—had I.

Even so, their doubts needled at me. On that last day, that final drive to the agency, I turned to Rachel. "You're not doing this just for me, are you?"

"What are you talking about, Aiden?"

"This baby. Would you prefer another, keep looking, wait a bit?"

"You're not getting cold feet, are you, babe?" she'd asked.

"No," I said, my voice thick as I stared at the black road, trying to concentrate. "I fell in love with her that first moment. But that's the problem. I didn't push you to her, did I? Drag you along?"

"Oh, Aiden," she said. "You couldn't drag me along if you tried."

I blinked, tried to keep the lines on the road from blurring. Of course I couldn't, my strong, willful wife.

"I'm in love with her too," she said. "And you."

Ours.

Gabby did have some problems. Intense colic followed by a couple years of broken bones. In her first two years, she broke her wrist twice, her foot once, and—for several long months of recovery—a femur. I was worried they'd think we were abusing her, take her away, but the doctor's bone scan revealed that her bones were more fragile than most. "What could cause it?" I'd asked.

"Probably poor nutrition—both prenatally and postpartum. A little neglect after she was born—too much time in a car seat, things like that. It's not uncommon with babies who are adopted out of stressful situations. But you got her young. A few adjustments to her diet and she should be fine."

"I hope her teeth are okay," Rachel said.

"Oh, a broken tooth isn't so bad," I said, flashing my own pearly whites. "Look what it gave me."

She leaned over Gabby's still-bald head, kissed me, right in front of the doctor.

"Yeah, she's going to be just fine," the doctor had said, laughing.

We put Gabby on a well-rounded diet with supplements of protein and calcium. Rachel spearheaded it, and I continued it after she was gone.

Even after her new, healthier diet, Gabby had still cried a lot, could sink into a mood with the slightest sharp word. I'd bowed to this poutiness. Rachel had not. "You've got to hold firm, Aiden. Otherwise, she'll learn she can manipulate us."

I wanted to reply that she *could* manipulate us— me anyway. Those eyes! But Rachel was looking a little glum herself lately, and I didn't push it. "Everything okay?" I'd asked.

"I'm just feeling a little under the weather," she replied.

"That's what you said last time," I said.

She paused. "Yeah, maybe I need an adjustment—more exercise or better food or something. Maybe Gabby and I both need some type of power diet."

She'd scheduled a doctor's appointment after that, planning to get a referral to a nutritionist. Rachel wasn't one to wait around for the stars to line up. She was a doer, a mover. Her doctor did a basic checkup, some routine bloodwork. And the rest, as they say, is history. He found lumps, some indicators in her blood. All the bad things that Rachel kept to herself, waiting to hear that it was no big deal. A little surgery, maybe a stint of chemo. Bad news, but not the worst. She hadn't expected a body shot through with cancerous bullet holes. She hadn't expected the life we'd finally gotten to get cut short. She hadn't expected to have to tell me.

The strange thing is that Gabby's moods got better after Rachel's diagnosis. She was learning to talk really well, and that must have helped. But there was something else, something about helping her mother. Gabby would pat Rachel's back every time Rachel hovered over the toilet to throw up. Just stand there, that little hand rubbing Rachel as she heaved. I'd never seen anything like it. Gabby started humming, just like Rachel had, and we played music more. They would both sing along, one dying, one with a second chance at life. I listened and danced Gabby around, holding Rachel's hand as she swayed along. Until she sat on the couch. Until she lay on the hospital bed in the living room. Her humming growing wobbly just as Gabby learned to twirl.

CHAPTER 29

PRESENT

I pick up a sandwich at the shop where I'd stopped with Nora. I avoid the turkey on rye, read the menu carefully, and somehow wind up with the tomato basil on focaccia that Nora had ordered last time. I want to regret it, but it's completely delicious and I'm starving. It's well past lunch, and I'd skipped breakfast worrying over the tow and everything.

My phone rings as I'm leaving the shop. Nora's voice. "Hey Aiden. I stopped in and Joe said you'd been by. More car trouble."

"Yup," I say.

She clears her throat. "Maybe next time you're in town, you should stop by. No pressure or anything, but—"

"Matter of fact, I did," I reply. "Met your roommate."

"Oh," she says. "Did she tell you I was out?"

"She invited me in," I say. "A couple of other guys were there too."

"That's…weird," she says, her voice a pause. "I was at the school studying for this bio test."

"That's great," I say.

"She was asleep when I got home. On the couch. I didn't think anything about it."

"I guess you didn't."

A flat line of silence on the other end of the phone. "Aiden, I—" Nora finally says.

"She was high as a kite," I say, in case it needs further clarification.

"She…" she says, "I—"

"No, it's fine. You don't have to explain yourself to me."

"No, I guess I don't, but—"

"But you really should get away. Like, all the way away. I don't know if you're doing that stuff too, or just turning a really blind eye, but—"

This time she interrupts me. "So since my room-mate was high, you assume I'm still on drugs too? After all I told you?"

"I'm not assuming anything," I say, though I am, did.

"Kind of seems like you are," she says. Her voice has shifted from worried to annoyed.

"Nora, I have a daughter. I can't take a risk like this."

"I wasn't aware that you were risking anything, Aiden."

Then why had it felt like I was—me going to her house, hoping to see her. "Well, I'm not."

"Clearly. Have a great day. I've got to get back to studying."

"Yeah. Bye," I say, and that's the end. I click my phone off, slam into my car and take off a little too quickly. *If you're even IN school,* I fume to myself, pressing the gas, accidentally blowing a red. The blue lights are flashing behind me in seconds.

I sigh, slow the car, and pull over.

"Aiden," Pete's familiar voice booms. "You again?"

"Can't seem to stay away," I say, holding out my license.

"So I hear," he says, waving my license away. "Small towns keep the news travelling fast. The juicier, the better. You coming from Joe's?"

"It's been a rough day. Had to get a tow."

"All the way down here?"

"It's cheap."

"And Joe's got a pretty receptionist." Pete taps

195

something into his computer. "You blew through that light kind of fast."

"Like I say, rough day."

"How's that little girl of yours doing?"

"Loving second grade, too much unicorn stuff," I respond as Pete hands me a slip of paper.

"Well, I'll tell you—it don't slow down none, so just enjoy those unicorns. I'm not gonna cite you or nothing, just a warning. Don't take it personally."

"No," I say. "I appreciate it. How's your boy?"

"Keeping his grades up. Met some girl he likes. It's like I said, time flies." He wipes the sweat off his forehead with his wrist. "Brace yourself, kid."

I smile and he taps the side of the door. "See you around."

"Probably not. Not anymore," I say.

"That bad of a day, huh?"

"That bad."

"Take care then. You still at Davis sometimes?"

"Every once in a while."

"Good man," he says.

I roll up the window as he walks away. Am I, I wonder. A good man?

My phone starts to ring before I can even get back on the road. "Hello," I snap to the unfamiliar number.

"Hello, Mr. Billings. This is Mrs. Naro, the school

nurse. We've got your daughter, Gabby, here in the office. She got a bit sick at recess."

I groan inside, check my watch. "I'm a ways out of town," I say. "I'll be there as soon as possible."

"How long do you think it will be?" she asks.

"I'm sorry," I say, "but at least forty-five minutes."

I can practically hear her sigh through the phone. "Okay, we've gotten her a new t-shirt. Her other one is here in a sack."

"That bad?" I ask, just like Pete asked me.

"It happens," she says.

I nod, though of course she can't see it. "I'm on my way," I say, connecting the phone to my Bluetooth and pulling into traffic. At least my car is purring like a kitten.

CHAPTER 30

SEVEN YEARS EARLIER

*J*n that manic week of prepping for baby, Rachel and I had bought a car seat, crib, two soft blankets, a few packages of onesies. We also had one frilly pink dress that Rachel's mom had sent. We felt like a strange mix of most prepared parents ever (we'd been waiting for over two years!) and least prepared parents ever (we'd gotten a baby in three weeks!).

Turned out new babies didn't care much for cribs, even if the blankets were soft. She baby-puked her way through all of the onesies in a day and a half, and went through twice as many diapers. Rachel didn't dare put her in anything frilly, dress or other-wise. The car seat, though—that was a hit. For the first three months it felt like the only thing that would put her to sleep. We spent countless hours walking, rocking, singing, and swaying. But driving was Gabby's true love, her only love.

Because of that, we spent a lot of time, late at night, sitting in the kitchen and gazing at her finally-sleeping face in that plastic car seat.

And what a face. Everything we'd wanted and a thousand times more.

Those emerald eyes, taking up half her head, a tiny pinch of a nose that hung over a pink heart of a mouth. Hands that grabbed and wrapped, erratically, anything they could hold—my finger, Rachel's hair, a fuzz ball from the carpet. Who knew parents cleaned so many fuzz balls out of their babies' tight fists? Who knew how many hours a parent could sit looking at those fists—the fingernails like delicate polka dots at the end of those pudgy fingers. When she screamed, her hands balled tight, scratching sometimes at her innocent face, her neck, our arms. But when she slept, the fists finally relaxed, easing open until you could slip a finger under the palm and she would close her hand around it.

What parent could ever have let go of such a hand? And yet I was grateful every single day for the birth mother who had let her go (okay, most days—we definitely had a few when both of us were trying to survive on only a couple hours of sleep, days when we nearly killed each other, when we thought of our old lives like shiny simple things that they never were). But those days winked out of my memory every night when we drove Gabby along country roads, then returned to our street, looking back under passing street lamps to see the cheeks relaxed, the head turned to the side, the arms splayed out like she was welcoming the whole world into them. More than one night, we didn't even move her, just leaned our car seats back for a few hours of rest before she woke, crying for her bottle. Then we would carry her in—the angel—dig up a bottle from the fridge, and stumble to our beds.

Rachel and I did not look any kind of cherubic. Rachel confessed that she'd gained fifteen pounds. My own pants were a little tight, but even worse than that was that every night, I left what felt like half my hair on my pillow. "Is it bald in back?" I'd asked Rachel. She'd run a hand through and tell me it still looked great. Maybe I wasn't bald, but I didn't look great. I only shaved now on the days I worked. The rest of the time, I let the stubble eat up half my face, tried to remember if I'd showered or not, and how long it had been.

The exhaustion didn't last, not forever. At fifteen

months, Gabby started to do something that resembled sleeping at night. She'd drop off at seven or so, usually on the couch or her bedroom floor where she'd been playing. We'd drop off too, into bed just minutes after she was asleep. No midnight snacks or afternoon delights. Sleep was serious business and we grabbed at it like drowning sailors. Gabby's three straight hours of sleep turned to five, turned to a full seven, though she was always up by four in the morning, ready to play. We'd take it. Rachel told me she'd lost weight and could fit into her favorite jeans again. I reintroduced myself to my razor each morning and stopped checking my head with a mirror, worrying I was going bald. My hair was there—maybe with a few extra grays. Rachel huffed that men could get away with gray anyway, and that was that.

Gabby didn't sleep past four in the morning until she started first grade when—cruelly—she suddenly decided she didn't want to get up in the mornings at all. All those pre-dawn years and suddenly I had to bribe her with hot chocolate and Cookie Crisp. Not the best method of parenting, but I was alone by that point and cookies in breakfast milk seemed a small price to pay for a morning of smiles instead of screams.

Her mouth had gotten bigger, though her nose was still a button of a thing. And those eyes—my first love, my Achilles heel—they still opened to the world like they had the first day we met. Wide oceans of wonder, mirroring back to me a lifetime of possibility.

CHAPTER 31

Gabby barfs for four days. The first day it happens every half hour. By the morning, her face is white, limbs limp. I nearly have to carry her to the toilet. In the bathroom, we sit together on the cold floor. I hand her the Gatorade. "I know you want to guzzle it, baby, but you just get one sip."

"But I'm so thirsty," she whispers.

"I know," I sigh, looking at her pale, dry lips. "But it doesn't do any good if you can't keep it down. One sip. I'll give you more every few minutes. Let's see if it helps."

It does. For several hours, she keeps the fluids down. After that, she barfs once more, but it's not too bad. She sleeps, wrapped into a ball on the couch. I crash too, sinking into my bed. It feels like about five minutes before she's vomiting again, but it's been six hours. I help her to the toilet, pour chicken soup from a can and warm it on the stove. "Best to get it down while you still feel okay."

Her eyelids droop, but she nods. "I'm hungry."

I'm glad to hear it but within an hour she's thrown it up.

"That's okay, baby girl. We'll keep trying."

"I don't want to try again right now," she says.

"Just Gatorade then," I say, and she sips.

By the beginning of day four, her stomach is flat and soft, but she asks for some food. I try toast this time. She eats, keeps it down. We go too adventurous at dinnertime with a bowl of Ramen. She stops eating halfway through.

"Too much," I say.

She nods, shuffling to the bathroom.

I can't say she throws up exactly. Just hovers over the toilet spitting and feeling lousy. At the end, she lies on the cold tiles, closes her eyes, and falls asleep right there.

In the morning, she pours herself a tall bowl of cereal.

"Gabby," I say with a warning.

"I'm soooo hungry," she says.

"I know," I begin. "Just…don't add milk."

It stays down, as does the toast for lunch. We try

more chicken soup for dinner. And then she's off, eating voraciously, back to school. I'm exhausted and take one final day off of work to get some sleep.

At lunch, when I go to get the mail, there's a bill for Joe's. It's about $200 more than I expected. *Nice.*

And just when I'm ready to shake off this whole horrible week, Nora calls. I don't answer, but I watch her name flash over my screen, then wait. Twenty seconds into thirty. I set the phone down, and it dings with the message. I look at it like it's a snake and I'm deciding whether to pick it up or not.

When I click the button, I hear her voice, a few simple words. "You were right. She was back on drugs. But she's gone now. See you around."

I play the message a few times, which seems silly. What am I expecting or wanting to hear? It was nice of her to call. Actually, it's always nice, the things she does. The cake, the candy jar, the way she remembered Gabby's name, how she helped me that first time at the tire shop.

"You were right," her electronic voice repeats. "But she's gone now." I wondered if the roommate had been arrested.

I play the message again, sitting on the couch, which is still covered with the sheet I'd used while Gabby slept there. "Back. *Back* on drugs." What did that mean exactly? Had they been friends before, done this type of thing together? I click the phone off, lean my head against the couch, fall asleep in less than thirty seconds.

When I wake a few hours later, my stomach doesn't feel so well.

I don't throw up nearly as much as Gabby did, only a couple of times. But I'm sick for a full week, no appetite or energy. I'm coming up on two weeks of sick days now, almost my entire allotment for the year.

CHAPTER 32

THREE YEARS EARLIER

*A*fter Rachel died. After Kate went back home to care for her own kids and family. After the meals brought by neighbors and the freezer meals left by Kate dwindled away. After several more months of frozen dinners and takeout nights, I stood in front of my empty fridge, empty freezer, cupboards with only a few odd things that only my late wife had known how to use; and I realized that I could either take Gabby out for every meal for the rest of our lives, or I could learn to cook. It wasn't something I looked forward to, not a natural gift, not even much of an inclination, but it was a necessity for both health and budget.

"What should we buy, Gabs?" I asked my almost four-year-old.

"Sketti," she replied. "Also, sandwiches. Also chicken." She'd recently embraced the word 'also' and used it every chance she got.

That was a start. I pulled up a page on my phone and wrote them down. Simple enough.

"Any fruits?" I asked.

I swear she rolled her eyes, even then. "Nanas," she said, like it was the most obvious answer in the world.

"Apples?" I asked.

"'Kay," Gabby said. "Also, smoomies." *Smoothies.*

At the end of Rachel's life, we'd made a lot of smoothies—special ones packed with calories and nutrition she would need, but couldn't eat because she was too sick and tired to get much down. She shared them with Gabby, just like any non-dying mother would have.

I googled a simple strawberry-banana smoothie, added frozen berries to my list. I tried to remember what I'd eaten pre-Rachel. Potatoes, eggs, bread and cold cuts. All those made the list, plus a few kinds of canned soup. Cereal. And in a final act of independence, a couple of bottles of grape juice. Rachel hadn't approved of sugary drinks of any kind, even when I'd made the argument about fruit. She would never have it. "Sugar's sugar," she'd said. "Your teeth don't know the difference."

When I was done, I added the grocery app to my phone and made an appointment to pick the food up.

Winning. I was winning at the dinner thing. First night, we had tomato soup and grilled cheese. Nailed it, except for one slightly burnt side on the sandwiches. Next night, smoothies and spaghetti, though Gabby complained that the smoothies weren't like Mommy's at all and that they had too many chunks.

Day three, I was determined to wow. I pulled out several frozen chicken breasts, a bag of frozen broccoli, and a block of cheese. "You like broccoli cheese casserole?" I asked.

"Not the *bwoccli*," she said. "Mama took mine out."

Not exactly true. She had just chopped the broccoli so small that it got into Gabby's mouth no matter how small the bites were. I learned that frozen broccoli didn't chop like regular broccoli. I learned that frozen chicken cooks better and faster when it's thawed. I learned that I had no idea how to make Rachel's cheese sauce (melting cheese was not the only step, like I'd thought). And when all was ruined and dinner was an hour late and tasted awful; and when we should have laughed and gone out for burgers, I pounded a fist onto the table, then chucked it all furiously into the garbage, which melted the garbage bag and made an even bigger mess. I swore. Gabby cried. No one ate, and I yelled that she had to go to her room while I figured it out. Which I didn't. I sat on the couch fuming, then limp, until the tears slowly crept out of my eyes. I wasn't even sure I'd call it crying. It didn't feel that way. It felt like everything just seeping out of me. I clicked an app and ordered a pizza, then sat on the couch staring at the TV I hadn't bothered to turn on. Gabby's crying stopped, but my face kept dripping. When the pizza guy got here, I grabbed a wad of tissues and fake sneezed so he would think I was sick or had allergies. I couldn't tell you what I tipped him; I hope it was decent. Then I called for Gabby. She didn't come down. I called again. No Gabby. Checked my watch. It was nearly 9:30. I went upstairs to find her asleep on the floor, curled into a blanket. She'd colored several pictures, then thoroughly coated her hand and arms and part of the floor with marker.

Oh Rachel, how are we going to do it without you?

I lifted Gabby into her bed, watching the angel face, smudged with black and green. Then I capped off the markers and took them away. I didn't want the pizza either, but I didn't throw it away. I shoved it into the refrigerator. The next night, when Gabby saw it, her eyes lit up. "Daddy, is this dinner?"

"Sure, sweetie."

We warmed it in the microwave and Gabby told me I was getting better at cooking.

"But I didn't cook it," I said.

"Mama bought pizza," Gabby said. "'Specially when dinner was yucky."

I laughed then. Finally. It'd taken long enough. "Yeah, I guess she did." I remembered them now. The failed vegan phase, the fish and chips she'd been so excited to try, the spicy Thai that almost burned our intestines out. "How do they have stomachs left?" Rachel had asked on Thai night, chugging milk, then clicking the app for pizza delivery. Pineapple and ham pizza that night. I didn't like it; Gabby did.

"What are you going to cook next?" Gabby asked, picking at a piece of pepperoni, then popping it into a chubby cheek.

"I don't know," I said. "What should I try?"

"Maybe macaroni," she said. "Mama was good at that."

"Mmmm," I replied, knowing I'd never master her family recipe.

"Also, white soup."

I nodded. Rachel's white chicken chili. I might be able to handle that one. Beans, chicken, milk, cream. We had over half a pizza left, so a backup plan if we needed it.

Another lesson from Rachel and Gabby. *Give it a try. And call for pizza if it doesn't work out. Then try again another night.*

I was pretty sure it was the kind of thing that applied to more than dinner.

CHAPTER 33

PRESENT

On that last day, home from work, nursing a cup of herbal tea, I call Nora. I don't know why. It'd be easier not to. It just seems kind of wrong to totally ghost her like that.

"Oh, Aiden, hi," she says when she picks up.

"Hey," I say, realizing that I sound kind of sick still. I clear my throat and try again. "Hey."

"You alright?" she asks.

"Yeah, Gabby got sick the day I went to Joe's, then I did. It's been an exciting couple of weeks."

She laughs. "Obviously." Then stops laughing. "I mean, I'm not laughing because I'm happy you were sick. It's just…I've been there too."

Now I laugh, and it feels good to break the ice. "No, I know what you mean. What have you been up to? Hopefully something better than barf."

"I mean, a little. Lost a roommate." She pauses, waiting for me to chime in.

"Yeah, I got the message. Did Pete come by?"

A confused silence on the other end of the line. "Pete?"

"A cop I know down there," I say. "But not him, I guess."

"No," she says. "No cops. Just...well, I turned her in."

"Turned her in?" I ask.

"Yeah." Another pause and I can imagine her fiddling with her fingers like she does. "This is kind of like a halfway house—I mean, not exactly, but there are rules we're supposed to keep. It seemed like kind of a jerk move to turn her in; I liked her. But, well, when you called, I realized that it would be easy to look guilty by association; and I'm supposed to be able to move out in another month. I even have a place picked out. I'd hate to have that pulled out from under me."

"Oh, wow," I say. "I'm so sorry. Sounds like a week of barf might have been simpler."

"Simpler, yes," she says. "But I'll still take the health. Meg—my old roommate—will be okay. It's hard to come clean, but it doesn't help if people are enabling you and stuff."

Now it's my turn for the awkward pause. I just

don't know what to say when the topic shifts to drugs or even recovery. So I shift it away. "Anything else new?" I ask.

"Yeah, actually. I've been working to get my driver's license."

I can hear the smile through the line. "That's awesome. You taking a driving class or something?"

"Nah, too expensive. A guy from Joe's has been teaching me. We drive every night."

"Oh," I say.

"Jason. Did you meet him?"

"Maybe." Blond guy, taller than I am, maybe a little younger too—closer to her age. "The blond guy?"

"Yeah, that's him. It's been really nice of him to teach me."

It seems bad that we're still talking about him. "That's great," I say. "I trust that you're a natural."

She laughs. "Jason says so, but it's a lie. I nearly hit a pole in the Walmart parking lot last night."

That's great, I almost say again, and then realize that it's the wrong thing. *Okay, have a great life,* also seems like the incorrect direction to go, so I just wait in a weird silence on the other end of the line.

"It's been nice to talk," she finally says. "I'm glad you called."

"Me too," I say, though I'm feeling a little sick again.

"See you around," she says, like she does.

"Bye, Nora." And then the line goes dead. I don't know why that fact makes me feel so sad. My tea's gone cold and I sit on the couch, swirling it around in the mug, thinking about her voice, the sway of her hair and hips, that other guy who's teaching her to drive and the way she must look so focused as she's learning. Her profile a mix of soft cheeks, determined eyes, pink lips, and the nose jutting out small and round. I tip back my cup, letting the lukewarm tonic slip down my dry throat.

*N*ora shows up on my doorstep a few days later. "I'm legit," she announces when I open the door. It takes me a minute to process the car behind her, that she's a solo driver.

"You did it!" I say and, without thinking, reach out and hug her. She hugs me back and halfway through, I start to wonder what I'm doing, holding this warm, soft creature when just two weeks ago, I was about to send the cops to her apartment. The hug suddenly feels like something I don't deserve. I pull away and she steps back.

"I brought this for Gabby, for the next time she's sick." She holds out a game, Connect Four. I remember playing it as a kid and realize that, aside from a few boxes of playing cards and some old partial puzzles, I have almost no games for Gabby.

"Thanks," I say, then call into the house for Gabby.

She pops her head around the hallway wall, like she'd been standing there waiting the whole time.

"Miss Nora brought this for you," I say.

"I heard you were sick," Nora adds, squatting down so she's at Gabby's level. "And I thought you and your dad might want to have something you could play together."

Gabby takes the box a little shyly, and then says, "How do you play?"

"Well, you put the chips into the columns." She points at the box, showing her the picture of black and red playing pieces. "And you try to stop the other person from getting four in a row." She looks at Gabby to see if she understands.

I cut in. "Maybe we should play a game." Just like the hug, I'm not sure where it's coming from. There's just something, and it's distinct, that doesn't want Nora to leave, not quite yet.

"Sure," Nora says.

Gabby leads her to the table and together they

break open the cellophane. Nora clicks the pieces together. I notice her arms, bare to the shoulders, the tattoos covering old marks, but no new needle pricks, no more secrets to hide. I open the little baggie with the black and red pieces and show Gabby how they slide into the slots.

For the next sixty minutes we laugh and block each other, or try to. I lose the most, but that might be because I sometimes let Gabby win. Nora doesn't. She's ruthless with Connect Four, tying Gabby at the end of the night. They both stare at each other over the board, both of them more competitive than I'll ever be. "Next time we'll break the tie," Nora says, "so you better practice with your dad."

Gabby grins devilishly, still staring, like she has every intention of practicing until she's the solo Connect Four queen, and then she quirks her head to the side. "Your eyes," she says, a sudden change to the subject. "They're just like mine."

"Green-eyed girls," Nora says, staring at Gabby, then tapping Gabby's nose. "Your mama must have been one too, since your daddy's are nearly black."

"Nah," Gabby says. "Mama's were brown, too. I'm adopted."

Nora laughs like Gabby is joking, then looks at me.

I nod slightly, so Nora doesn't accidentally say

something that will make both of them feel awkward.

"Oh, wow," Nora says. "How cool." She gazes at Gabby for another long minute, bats her eyes twice, then laughs. "Tell your daddy he's lucky you're not a redhead. They're nothing but trouble."

Gabby laughs. "You're not trouble."

"Hmmm," Nora says, tapping her cheek thoughtfully. "Trouble, that's another game we should learn to play."

"You know, I think I've got some ice cream in the freezer," I say. "You guys want some?"

"Yes!" Gabby shouts.

Nora glances at the clock in the kitchen.

I look at it too. Nearly eight. The night went fast. Gabby will have to go to bed soon. But maybe that's a good thing. Nora could stay. We could watch a movie. As I'm formulating plans, Nora is gathering up her things. "I think I'd better pass for tonight," she says. "Long drive back. And I'm still a rookie." She smiles.

"Thanks for coming up," I say. "It was just...really nice."

She smiles, me by the freezer, her by the table. And there's kind of this across the room thing that happens. "I'll walk you to the door," I say, setting the ice cream on the table and telling Gabby to grab a bowl.

I open the door for her, follow her onto my tiny porch. "That really was so nice," I say. "I appreciate it, and I know Gabby does to."

She laughs. "It's really no big deal," she says.

"It really is," I repeat.

"See you around, Aiden."

Our hands brush, and I take a finger, hook it into mine. "Hey," I begin, not really knowing where to go. "This was…" I'm about to say 'really nice' again and stop myself. "I had a good time. I'd like to…maybe do more."

"Are you sure, Aiden?" she asks. "I know I threw you for a loop with my past."

"Yeah," I say, answering both comments. I am sure, though she did throw me for a loop.

"I could come up again," she says, trying to keep her voice light, though her cheeks are pink, her finger still wrapped up in mine.

"Or I could take you to dinner sometime," I add. "Maybe this Sunday."

"Sunday is great," she says. "Should I come here?"

"No, no," I say, and suddenly my entire hand is wrapped up in those fingers. "I'll pick you up."

Her cheeks are on fire. And I like fire. "Okay," she says, her face tipped up. "Text me the time."

I lean in slightly, and we hang there, frozen for a second till Gabby bangs through the door. "Daddy, I spilled the chocolate sauce," she says, a quiver to her voice. "It's on the floor."

I break from Nora's hand, and as I do, Gabby seems to notice it.

"It's okay," I say. "We'd better go get it cleaned up."

Nora laughs, shaking the pink from her face with the sound. "Till Sunday. Bye, Gabby."

The pull of my daughter and the mess tug me back into the house, although I want to stand on the porch, watch Nora get into her car, drive back to her town. *I'm ready,* I think. Ready to get to know someone who isn't Rachel. Ready to move forward. Ready for a recovery story.

CHAPTER 34

FOUR YEARS EARLIER

*R*achel recovered from the chemo faster than I did. Kind of ironic, since I never had chemo, and since Rachel never recovered. But she just accepted it somehow—the fact that she didn't feel well, the fact that she was dying, the fact that her hair fell out and she had to draw dark lines of eyebrows over her eyes every morning, the fact that she could barely eat anything. When it got really bad, she asked me to make her rice almost every day. It was all she wanted to eat, plain and white. The stupidest thing was, I didn't even know how to make it. I'd been a bachelor for a while, but rice hadn't been my thing. I could bake a potato, grill every once in a while. I could even make a decent green salad. But that first week when she requested rice, I bought my wife—my dying wife—instant microwavable rice. Giving it to her that first time, it felt like one of the most shameful things I'd done. Shortly after, an ad popped up on my phone. A hundred dollar rice maker. I ordered it without a thought and when it came a few days later, I read the manual, set it up right next to her bed, and bought a bag of rice. She ate it with sugar and butter at first, and then with just sugar, then with nothing at all. Just a few bites at a time.

Two weeks later, she stopped eating altogether. Strange, these things; and the way they hurt.

I'd asked Kate not to sell the rice maker, back when she was clearing out. But I didn't use it that year, or the next year either.

Gabby had found it once, used it as a receptacle for dolls and ponies. Unaware that it had any purpose beyond Barbie habitation.

And then one day, we had a potluck for work. I remembered a recipe for a seasoned rice with veggies—something I'd only made once for Rachel, and it was too much—too many flavors, too many textures. We'd returned to white rice. But after I remembered, I re-read the recipe, chopped vegetables, added the dry seasoning. It turned out great. I fed it to Gabby the week after, and she liked it too.

Soon enough, the rice, and the rice maker, became a regular part of our weeks, our lives, sitting on the counter like it'd never borne the weight of a life unlived, like it'd never been more than a household appliance at all.

CHAPTER 35

PRESENT

They call us in for a structure fire. Could be anything from someone's garage to a hotel. The chief is already there, but the other volunteer has just pulled up in his truck. I open the garage, wave him over; and we're off. The fire could be in any part of the building. They've called for mutual aid—more fire, police, and EMS, so we'll get some help, but it might take a while.

I don't recognize the street name, but as soon as we drive into the neighborhood, I know it. The apartment is part of the complex where Nora lives. It's not hard to find the fire. Smoke is streaming out of one of the buildings—I'd guess third floor as the culprit—and dozens of people are standing on the lawn while others are rushing in and out of the building. One man helping an old woman with a walker, a middle-aged lady with an arm around a crying woman, two black teens helping a man who's coughing with a cut along his forearm. Helping each other like they do in tragedies like this. And then, there she is, Nora zooming around the building. She doesn't see me, probably wouldn't recognize me in my gear if she did.

The other firefighter is hooking up hoses while I gear up. A police officer tells us he's closed off the road and is filling the chief in on any details he knows. The medics arrive and are also touching base with the chief who's got a few people coughing outside the truck. As I pick up a hose, a man rushes forward with a burned hand, shouting something about a few kids he knows are inside.

The chief nods at me and I kick it into high gear, hurrying toward the building. One of the medics jumps out of the ambulance, and the scene swirls around me as my focus narrows.

"You know where any kids live?" I ask a woman who is rushing past.

"Upper floor, hon. Pretty sure an older woman lives there with her grandkids. I haven't seen none of 'em. Hoping they ain't home."

"You know what floor?" I ask.

"Three," she says and I thank her, telling her to stay back from the building. Blazes are starting to poke through a window where I thought we just had smoke. Not great. I run the steps, shove open the door to the hallway, not too hot. Smoke fills the hall, and I can see its source. I can also hear it because behind door 332, children are crying. The door is hot and I try the knob. Locked.

Halligan bar out. One thrust, then another. The lock is cheap and it pops open with ease. Outside, I can hear another unit arrive. Just in time. Two children are flat on the floor—maybe five and seven years old—sobbing.

"Is anybody else here?" I ask.

"The baby," one of them howls. "And gramma is in the kitchen."

I hope the other crew will hurry in, wishing I had eight hands instead of two when suddenly someone is beside me, reaching for the small hands, pulling them out the door. "Come on," a woman's voice says, soft-toned.

I look over to see Nora crawling along, scarf over her face. "Out!" I shout.

She grips the children's hands, leading them, crouched, down the hall.

I rush toward the kitchen where the flames lick along the walls and counters, out the window. A woman is on the ground, no pulse, no breath. Then I run back in toward the bedrooms. The smoke is bad and I crash into one of the rooms, see the crib. The child isn't crying, which is bad bad bad, but he has a pulse. I gather him into my arms and as I come out one of the other firefighters has arrived and is pulling the unresponsive woman along with him.

Outside the scream of water pummels the side of the building, the fire getting smaller, though the smoke is black and thick. We race to the stairwell, then down to the freedom of the lawn.

The medics are there and somewhere in the rush and thrust of it all, I process the other two children, still crying. Crying, when this one in my arms... All at once, he's not in my arms, taken away by one of the medics, along with the woman who is gray-faced and completely limp.

But moments like these don't spare time for thought. I'm back to the truck, to the hose. The grounds have been mostly cleared by the police department, the fire getting smaller, the sun clouded by the smoke that billows and billows until, finally, after time that seems both infinite and infinitesimal, it begins to thin. The charred walls, the dry air, the emptiness of an after-fire. Like we've been trans-ported to some ancient ruins, ruins that really took just minutes to create. People won't be moving back into this wing any time soon.

I remove my mask and helmet, wipe the sweat

that drips into my eyes, barely aware that my hair is soaked through, my undershirt too. The medics have left and I have no idea what happened to the woman or any of the children. We gather and clean. Police tape things off. And then I remember, Nora's hands, leading those children down the hall, her body bent in an awkward crawl.

"How many people got transported?" I ask one of the officers who passes by.

"Not sure. Quite a few, honestly. That one guy was burned from touching the doorknob of that apartment. Maybe. There were a few who'd inhaled too much smoke. Then the four from that apartment —the kids and that lady. Though only the baby and woman were really bad. If I had my guess, I'd say the old woman died before it even started; I'd say that's what started it in the first place. But just a guess; they'll know more in a few hours."

"Think the baby was alive?"

"They were working him."

That's all he says, but it's a good thing. If someone is well past saving, the medics won't work them. Of course, there are plenty of people they work who never make it, never find their own breath or heartbeat again. "What about the woman who took those other two kids out?" I ask.

The officer fans his face with his hat. "Didn't see

her go in one of the ambulances, so she's probably fine. Crazy girl—she shouldn't have gone in."

"You should have kept her out," I say. It's the wrong thing to say, on this scene that was chaotic and charged.

"Like I even saw her go in. There was a lot going on, kid. And people were helping. Sometimes we need that."

"She shouldn't have gone in," I say.

"She shouldn't have," he replies.

But what was he supposed to do? Arrest her? He's right; there was too much going on.

"She came out alright," he says. "Helped those kids."

I grumble a response. She'd helped me too. What would I have done if she hadn't been there? I would have taken the two kids and then gone back. But by the time I got back, I would have lost a few minutes; and minutes matter in scenes like these. She deserves some acknowledgment, a thank you.

I ignore the news vans that have piled around the scene like vultures, and trudge to the truck.

"You care if we swing around to the other side of the complex?" I ask. "I know someone who lives here. Want to check on her."

The chief shrugs a yes.

When we get to Nora's apartment, the door is

locked and I have to knock three times to get a response. She comes to the door with a towel wrapped around wet hair, though she still smells a little smoky.

When she looks into my eyes, I suddenly want to cry, have to breathe slowly to fight it away. I almost jump in and start scolding her for coming into the house, but she's looking at me with those eyes, green orbs just like Gabby's. "Thank you," I say.

She doesn't respond, doesn't even smile, hasn't stopped staring at me. "Aiden," she finally says, like it's a question. I realize my hair is matted with sweat and ash, my face pink, and I surely smell like a walking chimney.

"Yeah," I say. Then repeat, "Thanks. It was a big help, what you did. Dangerous, but...thank you."

She shakes her head like she's trying to process something. "It was you in the apartment."

"Yeah," I say again. "Thanks for taking those kids."

She nods like she's not processing what I'm saying, still staring. I've stripped off my overcoat, so I'm just there in pants, shirt, boots, and suspenders. Like I'm lounging around at the station, except a lot sweatier.

"I thought you worked in IT."

I laugh. She doesn't return it.

"I do this sometimes on the weekends," I say. "Used to work full time as a firefighter until Rachel died and I thought I should try something more sensible. Guess I'm not very good at sensible," I say, looking down at my dirty pants.

She's shaking her head in this strange, haunted way. "You never told me," she says.

"No," I say, feeling just a smidge like I'm in trouble, when I'm the one who was supposed to be in a burning building, not her. "We have a lot to learn about each other still."

She nods, but there are wrinkles along her eyes—deep lines of worry. My own smile closes off. I guess, like Kate, she doesn't think it's very responsible of me to gallivant off to dangerous fires. Looking down at my dirty clothes, feeling the grime on my face, it seems like they're both a little too right.

"See you around," I say, just like she always does. She doesn't reply. The chief is staring now, out of the window of the firetruck. It feels a little like he's my mom. "Bye."

"Bye, Aiden."

The click of a door.

I'm not surprised when she cancels for Sunday.

I am surprised when it's only a text. "I'm really sorry, but it's just not going to work out."

"For Sunday?" I text back. "We could try another day."

"It's not going to work out."

And that's all. So much for the whole firefighters wooing women thing. It obviously freaked her out. And, honestly, if she can't accept that part of me, then maybe it really isn't going to work out.

Which doesn't mean it doesn't sting a little, or confuse me a little, or make me just a little bit annoyed, her dropping it all like that. I try texting once more. "Something you want to talk about?"

She doesn't respond for several hours. I figure she isn't going to respond at all when my phone finally rings. I'm cleaning up the takeout Gabby and I had for dinner. "There are things I didn't tell you."

I wipe the counter, watch the rag move in circles like it's disconnected from me. "You could tell me now."

"I couldn't," she says. "Not like this, not over the phone. Besides, it really doesn't matter."

"What do you mean it doesn't matter?" I ask, the

rag stopping, a limp, grungy thing. "Seems like it matters quite a bit."

"It does," she says. "Too much."

"Just tell me," I say. "Heal the wound, or rip the Band-Aid off. Either way is better."

"I wish all wounds could heal," she says. And then hangs up.

Is it wrong to be mad at the person who helped save a couple kids' lives, the woman I wanted to take to dinner, the one I'd started fantasizing about kissing? Because I'm super ticked. I click off my phone, bang dishes into the dishwasher, glad for once that Gabby will watch YouTube without coming up for air. By the end of the night, the kitchen is shiny and my boil has turned to a slow, solid simmer. Good riddance to her. If she's going to keep things from me, if it's all too big to talk about. Maybe it is, with all her issues. I'm glad she's in another town, another life, that I never have to see her again.

CHAPTER 36

PRESENT

*R*achel's wedding ring sits in a black velvet box at the back of my closet. I'd planned to buy her a solitaire, big and bright. She'd asked for a gold band, said that she worked all day in latex gloves, that solitaires tore them. Most of the women at the office didn't even wear their rings. She wanted to—that's what she said. So I found a gold band, vines etched all around it. Something she could wear all the time. Something I thought would symbolize life, longevity, those vines twisting. Around and around.

I close the box.

CHAPTER 37

PRESENT

The good news: All three children survived, even the baby. I'm ecstatic when I hear.

The bad news. I'm going to have to see Nora again. News 44 is doing a special interest story. Somehow they got Nora's name; and mine. They want an interview.

I show up at the news studio thirty minutes early, as instructed. It's not a huge affair in this small Kentucky town, but I've never been on television before and I'm already sweating. They usher me into a waiting room where screens hang from the walls with the live news on some and the scrolling words of upcoming stories on others. A woman takes my name, invites me to sit. Nora arrives about five minutes after me. She's wearing black slacks with a pink blouse that flows over her arms, hiding the tattoos, as well as sharp heels she seems a little unsure of. The woman introduces us, assuming that we don't know each other. Then, with honest tears in her eyes, the woman says, "This must be such a moment for the both of you, saving those kids together."

I smile and hope it doesn't look forced, that it doesn't give anything away. Nora's face is open and warm. "I'm so glad they lived," she says, and the woman wanders away, dabbing her eyes as another guest enters the waiting zone.

Nora clears her throat. "Hey."

"How's it going?"

"It's going well," she answers and I note the formal grammar.

"Thanks for your help on that scene," I add. "It was really tense and you were brave."

"Everyone was brave," she answers. "Everyone in the whole complex helping out. A beautiful thing really."

"Only you went in." And when I say it, I hear the accusation in my own voice. *You shouldn't have done that. It was dangerous.* I notice, too, the irony of the accusation. She's not the one with a seven-year-old daughter.

Nora shrugs. "I figured I owed a little something to the world."

It's not what I expect to hear and I don't have a response. A young guy in super skinny jeans comes over and shows us to another waiting zone, just outside the newsroom. He hands us microphones, shows us how to thread them through our shirts, clip them onto our necklines. Then he instructs us to speak while he listens in with headphones. He makes a small adjustment to mine and then quietly ushers us into the final room. "You guys are up in ten minutes. Wait here and you can watch the tail end of the story before."

It's a chef demonstrating a billion ways to cook squash. Nora watches with rapt attention, her profile a solid line against the black wall behind us. The chef finishes and the host—Mary Ellis, a celebrity here in Davis County—takes it away, a screen scrolling text in front of her. "Up next, we get to meet two of Davis's hometown heroes. Nora Evans and Aiden Billings—a citizen and a firefighter who worked together to save three children from the Maple Street apartment fires last week. After the break."

She sighs and leans back on her white couch as the screen scrolls continuously. She must be close to fifty years old, but thin and fit, black coils of hair against a smooth chocolate face. Plump lips, lined eyes, a few soft wrinkles that only enhance her beauty somehow. Up close I see a few dark freckles. She stands and gestures us over. "So good to meet the both of you," she says and another screen rattles on with an ad about laundry detergent. "This is the type of story that makes my job worth doing."

The skinny jeans tech is back, showing us where to sit. We're positioned next to each other and he nudges me a little closer so that we're both nicely in the frame. Nora is visibly shaking and I feel a small pang for her.

"Nervous?" Skinny Jeans asks.

"You have no idea," Nora says.

Mary smiles, all those white teeth, then pats Nora's hand. "No reason for nerves, baby. I'll just ask a few questions and we'll chat. It'll feel like seconds."

Nora nods, but doesn't answer.

"Besides," Mary says as the commercial winds down. "You guys look like movie stars on that couch. I might as well be interviewing Brad Pitt and Angelina Jolie. You know, if they still wanted to sit next to one another."

Nora blushes just as someone behind the camera begins to count down. Mary faces the camera, that big smile opening up as the camera man hits one and points.

"We're back with Nora Evans and Aiden Billings, two heroes from last week's fire at the Maple Street apartments. Aiden is a volunteer with the Davis Fire Department and Nora a resident of the apartments. Now, Aiden, I understand that when you first got to the scene there were already quite a few residents helping out."

"Yes," I say, finding my voice. "A lot. They were leading people from the building, holding kids who were scared, that sort of thing. It's something that happens often in a scene like that—everyone helping out. No one cares all of a sudden who you voted for, or how much money the other guy makes."

"And you, Nora?" Mary says. "When did you know what was happening? How did it feel to know part of your own apartment complex was on fire?"

Nora pauses and I hold my breath. Her cheeks are still pink. A second passes, then another. Mary holds the smile. "I..." Nora begins and I exhale. "This is going to sound weird, but it didn't feel like my building was on fire. It just felt like...I don't know; it's hard to explain. I smelled the smoke, heard the sirens. People started running. I could hear them, which sounds funny because it was an entirely different part of the complex and there was so much noise, but that's what I remember, the sound of running. And then I knew it was a fire. I wanted to hide in my room, which sounds a little crazy, I guess. And then I heard a woman crying and—I don't know—all of a sudden I was there, outside, leading people out."

"It must have been terrifying," Mary says, leaning forward, her own cheeks flushed like she's caught in the moment.

"I didn't feel afraid then. It was like something else just took over and I knew I could help. A fire-fighter went in." She nods to me. "And I followed. I didn't even think about it."

"Don't try that at home," I say, laughing into the camera. "It was a dangerous move, but I'd just pulled a couple kids from the fire and knew there was another in the building. I couldn't take all three. Nora showed up just in time to lead the two I had in the hall out of the smoky building. Which allowed me to get the last one."

"Amazing," Mary says, leaning back. "Just amazing. And how did you *know*?" she asks Nora.

"I didn't," Nora replies. "I just felt. And moved. I guess it was dangerous, but someone might as well have been pushing my back. I knew I had to go in. I knew—" She stops talking, looks to me, then Mary. "It just felt right and I wanted to help."

But I know—know what she didn't say. That it felt like she'd been guided, like she just knew the right thing to do. I'd felt it before on calls, something primal and instinctive, maybe even holy—I don't know. Whatever it was took over and you did what was right, even though if someone had asked you what was right before the call, you would have said something else.

Mary is talking and I miss it. Nora nudges me. "Aiden got the baby," she says.

"It was scary," I say. I can tell by Mary's face that I'm answering the right question and that's good. "I wasn't sure if he would make it. He didn't look good. And I thought maybe it'd all been a waste, Nora's risk in the building, me going back, but then—" I'm surprised at the choke of my voice, clear it, finish. "He lived." I smile. "Huge shout-out to the medics who helped him, and all the doctors and nurses."

"Beautiful," Mary concludes. "Thank you both." The screen rolls to a commercial, and it really does feel like it's only been a few seconds of airtime.

Nora and I both take a deep breath, let it out, and then I ask, "Does anyone know what's going on with the kids?"

"The baby is still in the hospital—improving every day, and the other two children are currently being cared for by a family in the area," Mary answers.

My face goes slack. Foster care, they're in foster

care. The grandmother died, was dead already. I hold my expression in what I hope is neutral.

Mary reaches out, takes both of our hands. "You two are just amazing. Thank you."

"Anyone would have done it," I say.

Nora nods. "They would have. Like I tried to say, you couldn't not do it."

Mary raises an eyebrow and squeezes our arms with her soft fingers. "Well, I think it's remarkable."

"So the kids are in foster?" I ask. "The grand-mother died?"

Mary nods. "Truly, the whole community has come together."

"Hopefully they find someone who can take them all on a more permanent basis," I say.

"We're hoping," Mary replies. "I imagine they're looking into options with family members. These things take time." We're ushered off the couch and a woman from the zoo holding a parrot takes our place.

"I applied," Nora says as we both go through the double doors, through another room, and out to the parking lot. "For fostering."

"You did?" I ask, a little stunned.

"Rejected," she says. "My history."

"It's okay," I say, stopping myself before adding more, before saying that they'll do better in a bigger home with someone who can keep all three, who has a more solid job, who isn't in night school. I say simply, "Give yourself a few more years."

"Thanks, Aiden," she says, stopping by her car. The green eyes, the simple smile. "I even bought a car seat."

I see it in her car, watch her open the door, touch the handle of the car seat. And then I see something else. The crook of her arm, the needle scabs like there aren't tattoos. The posture, the figure. A ragged tank top instead of a pink shirt and business slacks. The eyes cast down, so I couldn't see their color. That awkward moment when Gabby told her she was adopted. Nora's shock when she found out I was a firefighter. "No," I whisper. "No no no no."

Nora looks up, those green eyes now making eye contact with mine. She knows I know. "It's been good to meet you, amazing to see Gabby. You're a great father." She slips into the driver's seat, turns on the engine, backs away.

I can't move. I watch her drive all the way out of the parking lot before I realize that I'm still standing there, that I'm crying.

---

*W*hen I get home, Gabby hops around. "I saw you! On the news!" Natalie comes in.

"You sounded great," she says. "I didn't realize you volunteered on the side."

"Yeah," I reply. "Getting a little old for so much excitement though."

"Didn't look like it," she says, that coy voice. I look at her and see that she thinks something of me and Nora. Maybe Gabby told her.

"Thanks for taking care of Gabby," I say to Natalie.

"Anytime," she replies, headed for the door. "The girls had an awesome time together."

I open the door for Natalie, watch her sashay away with her daughter. Why couldn't I have fallen for her instead? A divorcée, simple, nice, my kids' friends' mom.

Gabby's bouncing on the couch. "Let's watch it again!" she nearly shouts.

"I don't know," I reply. "I'm a bit tired."

"Were you scared of being on TV?" she asks.

"A little nervous."

"Did they put makeup on you? Lacie says they put makeup on you, even the boys."

"Nope, they didn't," I answer.

I plunk down at the table and she sits across from me, gazing into my eyes. "Why are you sad?" she asks.

"I'm not," I say. "Just a big day. A big, crazy day. Let's get pizza for dinner."

"'Kay," she answers.

I lean forward. "Want to try a staring contest?"

She giggles. "You never win."

I gaze into her eyes, her perfect eyes, unblinking. She stares back, all determination. Green green green with a stroke of hazel through the left. Eyes I fell in love with the moment I saw them from that second-hand car seat. I close my eyes and she laughs.

"Told you," she squeals. "I win."

*K*ate calls just as the pizza arrives. "You're still working!" she shouts so loudly that I have to move the phone away from my ear. "You said you weren't working!"

"I never said that," I say, grabbing a slice of pizza and heading out to the patio to talk to her alone.

"You said you turned in your uniform," she spits.

"I did."

"And then got another job!"

"It's volunteer," I say.

"Who freaking cares?" she says, barely checking her language, so that I know her kids are around.

"It's usually slow," I say. "Only once a month."

"Wasn't slow last month."

"Look, Katie," I say, flopping my pizza onto the dirty patio table. "I'm tired. And I have a right to do what I want."

"But you HID it!"

What can I say? I did. Maybe we all have secrets —things so close we're afraid to share.

"Aiden, you can work anywhere you want. Really. Do whatever. But next time tell me."

"I know," I say.

"You mean, 'I will.'" The mother in her coming through.

"I don't know what I mean."

CHAPTER 38

PRESENT

o memories left. I lie in a lonely bed, the same one I shared with Rachel. Tonight it feels like a black hole. Why, why of all the people in the world, all the druggies, all the birth mothers? Why'd it have to be Nora?

INTERLUDE

NORA

I was gonna get an abortion. It was the logical thing, right? But whether I was too irresponsible or depressed or maybe I just sensed something bigger than myself was growing deep in my belly—at any rate, I let the months roll away without doing anything, anything at all.

By the time I plunked my butt down at the free clinic, I was six months along. "What do I do?" I asked the ample black woman who was wrapping a blood pressure cuff around my arm.

"Well, baby child," she said, sweeping my hair out of my eyes. I still remember the way she did it—efficient and tender all in one movement. "You have you a baby."

"I can't," I said.

She laughed at that—a big belly sound. "Oh, you can," she said. "And you will."

"But how?" I asked.

She quieted down, sat in the stool beside me pumping up the cuff. "All this talk ain't good for the numbers on the cuff, baby, now hush."

I hushed. She nodded at the blood pressure cuff, listening through her stethoscope.

Finally, she unwrapped my arm. "Skinny thing, ain't ya. You taking anything?"

I didn't answer.

"Any medicine?" she clarified.

I shook my head.

"Well, don't take nothing else either. Nothing more than a Tylenol."

I nodded. I'd been clean since I found out. I knew that much mattered. But being clean had left me exhausted, and I'd spent almost every day watching TV until the power had gone off, probably because the electric hadn't been paid again. Before that, well, that was just a blur of nights awake picking and pacing and long sleeps in between when I came down. Screaming. Lots of that too. Always lots with him, with Clive. Stomping, throwing things. He used to pull my hair.

I wince at the thought, put it down like I've learned to do, imagine a soft hand patting my head.

Imagine the swoosh of that black nurse's hand across my forehead.

I was super clean after that visit—not even a little sip of beer. I slept through most days, too depressed to move. Got a temp job at an office. Lost it in two days when I didn't show up.

Clive was gone most of the time. And that was good. He'd pop in Monday or Tuesday, raid the drawer for money. Usually nothing. Then leave again.

"You got fat," he said one day. And that was the only nod he gave to the pregnancy. Maybe he hadn't even noticed. He had another girlfriend by now, probably in some other trailer. *I* noticed that. The cheap perfume smell in his hair and clothes. And he had to be going somewhere.

I picked up food once a week at the food bank, ate mostly pasta and tuna. I was at the food bank the day my water broke. Looked up at the lady behind the counter.

"You okay?"

"Baby," I whispered, holding my belly. She looked at it, crossed herself, and called an ambulance.

One slender guy. One heavy. "You're not gonna have that baby on this ambulance now, so don't you worry," the skinny one said, talking nonstop. "No siree. Not here. Me and Will, we got a perfect record.

Always get 'em to the hospital on time, don't we Will?"

From the driver's seat Will only grunted. That's what I did too. Grunting and breathing. A big fat pig stuck in mud.

"Not had a baby on the ambulance yet," Skinny continued, opening a kit for babies and taking out a pair of scissors like he was a whole lot less confident about his perfect streak than he let on.

But they did get me to the hospital—Skinny and Will. Rolling me in like a Mama-pig queen. They stopped me in front of a woman who asked so many questions it kind of seemed like I should have gotten my GED by answering them all.

I didn't.

I got a frowning nurse and a cold gown. And after nine more hours of grunts and pushes and poop, I got a pink lump of baby placed on my chest.

I knew then that I would raise her right, be the perfect mother, shape up, give her everything I'd never had. She'd know love and a woman who swept her hair off her face. She'd learn to read and get straight A's and maybe in the summer we'd take a trip to somewhere with flip-flops and tourist shops, though I couldn't quite picture where.

A whole new life, it would rise up for the two of us out of the perfection that was this child.

In the end, I guess that was true, a promise I kept. Just not quite the way I'd planned, not quite the way I'd meant. Back then, I figured I could try the temp agency again—one no-show was okay, right? Then I'd make the payment on the trailer lot; it was only a couple months overdue, and Clive would move in with that other woman. I had an application for food stamps sitting right on my floor—the neighbor had brought it, along with a bag of her old maternity clothes a few months back. It'd work out. Anything could work out if *he* was gone. And he was. A new girlfriend for him. A new life for me. Perfect.

My two days at the hospital really were perfect.

I barely noticed the sideways looks the nurses gave me, the scribbles of notes they felt compelled to add to my chart.

I named her Rose. I was supposed to fill out some paperwork about a birth certificate, but I ignored it and stuffed it in a free diaper bag they'd given me with an army's share of formula and a few bottles. I'd fill the paper out later when I'd settled on a middle name.

That afternoon, my nurse—a tiny blond, probably shorter than five feet, asked who was coming to drive me home.

"Nobody," I said.

"You'll need a car seat," she added, making a note

on her clipboard. "Otherwise, you can't leave."

"I'm walking home," I said. "Ain't far."

"*Ain't* it?" she asked and the way she said it sounded like I'd done something wrong. "You'll need a car seat either way."

"Now that don't make sense," I said.

"Got to get it approved too."

"Well, I ain't got one," I said.

"Ain't ya?" she said, smacking her lips in a way that made me want to slap her.

That afternoon, a sweet lady from some kind of charity showed up in my room. She talked on about nursing though Rose was happily sucking a bottle at the time. They'd glued a bow on her bald head and I couldn't stop thinking how precious it was. I didn't hear much till charity lady said something about a car seat.

"Ain't got one," I interjected.

She cleared her throat in this soft way, like she was a lady who'd never picked a scab in her life. "It's the law," she said.

"Ain't got a car neither."

She nodded, made a note in her little flowery book. "We'll see what we can do." She patted my knee and I thought that maybe that's what a grandma would do if I'd ever had one I could remember.

Discharge morning the short blond nurse showed up with Flower Notebook and even though it seemed the nurse was gritting her teeth the whole time, Flower Notebook pulled out a small pink car seat.

"Transport's taking you home," the blond said.

"I can walk," I repeated, though I was still bleeding like a volcano.

Flower Notebook shook her head. "They'll take you, hon. Right to your house."

I nodded.

"Do well," she whispered to me as I climbed into the thing that looked like a miniature ambulance.

New baby, new car seat, new life.

When we got to the trailer, the driver didn't help us out. That was fine by me. I opened the screen, pushed through the door, then stopped. Four paces in. Clive was sitting on the couch, high as a kite, both legs shaking, eyes dilated.

"I missed you, baby," he said, and I looked down at the car seat, though I knew that wasn't who he was talking to. The other woman must have broken up with him. All my walls, they closed in just like on the movies.

I lasted six days sober. He went out; he came down. On day six, he chopped the line up, right in front of me while Rose was drinking her bottle.

"Ain't good for the baby," I said.

"She don't even care. Look at her. Besides, it'll give you energy for some of the stuff you got to do."

That much was true.

He rolled a paper, snorted the line. I swear my mouth watered, skin prickled.

He rolled another paper, shoved it into my hand.

"It'll shut off the blood," he said.

Just a breath of it, that's all I'd need.

It was more than a breath, that snort of powder, the energy that seared into my veins. I couldn't see anything but the energy, orange and hot and beautiful.

"Feels good, don't it?" he asked.

And dang if it didn't.

I'd been so tired, all those months and nights pregnant, all those days since Rose's birth. Now energy throbbed into my stretched and released body. We didn't sleep, eat, talk. But the next day, or was it night—time got lost to me when I did a line. Whatever time it was, he was back to screaming and cussing. The baby was crying. I fumbled with the tiny diaper, tried to get the Velcro things to stick. He threw a plate into the sink; it shattered. Then he stumbled to the table, pulled out his pocketknife, nicked the wood over and over, his way of picking.

"Shut. Her. Up."

I lifted the car seat—her diaper was still sagging —swung it back and forth. She cried harder. The milk or whatever it was that remained in my breasts seemed to swell, and I realized that my bleeding hadn't stopped either, that in fact, it only seemed to have gotten worse. My legs shook, arms shook, everything shook. He stabbed the pocketknife into the table and lurched up.

Books. That's what babies liked. I set her down, fished out a book from the bag they'd given me at the hospital. Thick cardboard pages. Perfect for babies.

He fumbled for the crack pipe, loaded it with yellow crystals.

I opened the book, recognized the caterpillar from my own childhood. Little Rose wailed. He jerked me back by the hair and I dropped the book, right on her forehead.

"Get her out," he screamed.

I shuffled and crawled, grabbing a hat, lifting her up in that heavy car seat, feeling the blood ooze out of me.

Nighttime. It was night. The minutes blurred, and then he was asleep, the pipe forgotten at a spot on the end table.

I'd meant to walk back to the hospital, find Flower Notebook maybe, but first I'd stopped at the

Chevron Station, bought a Hershey bar, tried to collect my thoughts. They resisted collection, scattering and flinging about. My head hurt from him pulling, from the line—my first in months, and from something so deep I couldn't even look at it. *Get her out.*

I unwrapped the Hershey bar in the parking lot, dropped the wrapper, and looked up to see the sign. A literal sign. In the form of a billboard. It loomed over the road. *Crisis? Surrendering your Newborn at a Fire Station Delivers... No Shame. No Blame. No Names.*

I looked at the crisp arch of bruise that had popped out on her forehead, then down at my shaking hands. And I did something I've never regretted though I'll always regret it every day of my life.

Half a mile.

I could walk that, even with the blood squishing in the pad, even with my hands shaking from the leftover high, even with my arms burning from the weight of that pink car seat.

I could walk 3,000 feet down a concrete road in the middle of the night with my little baby Rose.

And I did.

CHAPTER 39

PRESENT

*I*n the morning, my chief calls. "Hey, Aiden. Saw the story on the news."

"You should have been the one on the news," I reply. "You're the guy in charge."

"Nah," he replies. "I mean, I am the guy in charge." He laughs. "But you're the one who saved those kids."

"You know just as well as I that I didn't *save* anyone."

"I don't know," the chief says. "I'd call this a pretty decent save."

I grunt. Saving sounds gallant, but it's always a team effort—us, the medics, even the patients themselves—we all need to be part of it.

"News story was nice too. Good PR."

I can feel the smile in his voice, try to return it. "Yeah, thanks."

He hesitates, does a little thing with his throat. "And that girl," he says.

For a minute I think he means one of the kids we saved, but then he goes on. "The one on the news. Nora, they said her name was. Pretty good-looking. Sweet voice too."

I remember that he's been divorced for a couple of years. "Yeah," I say.

"Did you get to know her at all?" he asks, then laughs at himself. "I know it's a long shot but I'd love to have her phone number, maybe even an introduction."

Now it's my turn to hesitate, although I don't understand why. The chief's a nice guy, and Nora deserves that. "Actually, we did exchange numbers. Just friendly," I add quickly. "Hang on a second."

I give him Nora's number, but I know I don't have it in me to do a real introduction. "Just tell her that Aiden gave it to you."

"Awesome, man. Thanks."

"No problem," I say. But when I hang up the phone, I can't find the shirt I was going to iron; or the socks I was going to wear. After tearing every piece of clothing out of my closet, I find the shirt hanging over my shoulder. The socks are still in the drawer; I'd never taken them out. My wallet is on the dresser, but I wander around for at least five minutes looking for the keys.

"Gabby," I holler. "We've got to go. I'm running late." She comes downstairs in a unicorn-worthy outfit. Rainbow pants with a neon green and pink shirt that says, "Girls rule." Kate must have bought that for her. Her hair hasn't been brushed, but I don't have time to worry about it. "Into the car, sweetie."

"Can you braid my hair?" she asks.

"Not today, little girl."

A dramatic sigh.

"Bring your hustle," I say, scooting her toward the door, noticing that she's wearing her gold sparkly sandals, even though it's supposed to be in the forties today. "Socks," I mutter, turning around. "Also, coat." A second-grader might get away with a blindingly colorful outfit, maybe even gold shoes, but I don't want to get a call about her not being able to go to recess because she's not got a coat.

I hurry through the front room, turning over pillows and searching for her coat.

"Daddy," she says, that voice still holding the dramatic sigh. "It's right *here.*"

She's lifted it off the hook.

I shuffle back, throw open the door, and practically shove her out. I'm definitely going to be late.

"Daddy!" she wails, looking down at her shoes. One of the straps has broken.

Unlock the door, push her back in. "Quickly," I growl, cursing under my breath.

She comes back to the car approximately seven hundred hours later wearing flip-flops. "Nope," I say, rushing inside with her. "You're not even allowed to wear those at school. You know that."

"They're all I could find," she whines.

My curse is no longer under my breath. I drag her inside and up to her room. No wonder she can't find anything. It's a total disaster. Clothes and shoes and toys all over the floor so that I can hardly walk. "Gabby," I say. "This is not okay. You'll have every inch of this cleaned up after school before you do a single other thing."

And then the wailing. I throw my head back, like I'm staring at the heavens, though it's really just a little girl's ceiling, which needs another coat of paint. "Shoes," I demand, and we start digging through the piles. At least I start digging. Gabby stands there sniffling.

"Move!" I shout.

It doesn't work. She just sits in the mess.

"Gabby, I am LATE for work, and you don't have any shoes. This room is a mess. Please help me."

She pushes a few dirty leggings to the side, stares

at the carpet like some shoes might appear there. I whip out a ratty pair of tennis shoes and hand them to her. "Done," I say.

"But these are ugly," she whimpers.

"You loved them," I reply. "That's why we bought them."

"Ugly," she repeats.

"Too bad," I say, stuffing her feet into them. She's not helping, her legs limp as I fight her into them. Snot is dripping onto her lip and I grab a wad of tissues as we make our way back to the front door.

When we're finally buckled, I look into the rearview mirror. We make quite the pair, me in a wrinkled shirt, my daughter wearing mismatched clothes, her fine hair frizzed and probably knotted at the back, the tear streaks, the tissues shoved against her nose. I should laugh. I don't.

"Oh, Gabby," I say, imagining for one brief minute that this would all be better if Rachel were still here. Maybe it would be, but I know we had crazy mornings then too, angry ones, lost socks, plenty of tears—usually from Gabby, though not always.

I turn the key in the ignition and the engine gives a weak attempt at starting. I close my eyes, lean back against the headrest.

"Daddy?" Gabby sniffles from the backseat.

"Hang on, baby," I say, punching the number into my phone. "Going to be late," I grumble at the receptionist. "Battery dead."

"Don't you have that call with a client at nine?" the receptionist asks.

Yup, I sure do. "Can you reschedule it for an hour later?" I plead in my nicest voice. "I just need to get a jump."

She sighs, just as dramatically as Gabby did, and I remember why I'm never late. "I'll try," she says.

"Thanks," I mutter, getting out of the car and opening the trunk. The jumper cables are beneath two lawn chairs, an old blanket, and my jump kit for the fire department.

"Daddy?" Gabby says again, scooting out of side of the car. "What's wrong?"

"Battery's dead," I say shortly.

She nods like that's something she understands.

"I'll see if the neighbor's left for work," I say.

"We could call Nora," she says. "She got a new car."

I stop, turn to look at her. "She lives too far away."

"But she'd probably come," Gabby adds.

"Not in time," I say. "I've got an important call this morning."

"She could be here by ten," Gabby insists.

"Honey," I say. "She has work, other responsibilities. We couldn't call her."

"Did you break up again?" she asks. "Sammy broke up with Lila three times."

"We weren't dating, baby." I open the hood, connect the red, let the black side dangle.

Gabby comes over to watch.

"Don't touch," I say.

She puts her hands in her coat pockets. "Why'd she come so much if you weren't dating?" she asks, staring at the engine.

"I don't know. We were friends, I guess," I say.

"Then she would come."

"Gabby."

"Friends come if you ask," Gabby says, a little pout to her lower lip. "Maybe she could come tonight and fix your car for good."

It should make me laugh. Instead I just say, "Probably not tonight. Or any night." I look down, texting my neighbor.

Gabby reaches out to touch the battery.

"Do. Not. Touch," I say.

"It's not hot," she says, pulling her hand back. "Why won't Nora come?"

"She's just got some stuff to deal with, that's all."

"What stuff?"

The neighbor isn't texting me back. I look down the road, searching for cars still in their driveways.

"Just some mistakes she made when she was younger," I say.

"Miss Farr says we make mistakes to learn from them. Did Nora not learn?"

"She did, I think. She just…It was big stuff."

"I'm sorry, Daddy." Gabby plops down on the curb. "I hope she learns if she didn't."

"She did," I say, tapping the hood. "I didn't mean…"

She had learned, started a new life, gotten a job, gone back to school. A sapling growing in the ashes after a forest fire. And she'd been honest with me the whole time, telling me more than I ever had a right to know.

Maybe she wasn't really the one who had stuff to deal with.

A car comes down the road, slows when it sees me standing there with the hood open. The guy rolls down the window. "Need a hand?"

"Don't we all, man," I say. He smiles, pulls up in front of me.

Within minutes, Gabby and I are on the road.

"Oh, look," she says, a smile lighting up her voice. "My shoes. The pink ones." She stretches down and lifts the pretty shoes off the floor of the car. "I guess today worked out after all. Right, Daddy?"

I check the clock. Just a few minutes after nine. "I guess it did, baby. I'm sorry I yelled earlier."

"'S'okay."

"You've still got to clean your room though."

The dramatic sigh. She hops out of the car, walks like a rainbow-adorned '80s pop star into her school. But that's not what I see. I see a sapling. Growing in the ashes after a forest fire. A whole forest of saplings pushing up through the dust.

CHAPTER 40

PRESENT

I head into the grocery store, straight for the flowers. Maybe it would be classier to go to a florist, but Rachel was never picky about that stuff. In fact, she would have been annoyed if I'd dropped a hundred bucks on flowers. Especially now. I choose a nice autumn assortment, some mums and daisies, a few yellow and red roses, something green that smells almost minty. The woman at the checkout asks if I want a card to go with it. I pause at the question, then shake my head. It's been a while since I've done this ritual. Too long.

The flowers match the setting sun as I make my way out to the country. Oranges and yellows, white rays of sun stretching through the clouds. Hills roll up and open for me. A short gravel road. And I'm there. The cast iron gates hang open, regal and fore-boding as always.

Sunrise Cemetery. The last time I came was with Gabby, on what would have been Rachel's thirty-fifth birthday. Eight months ago. I straighten my collar and step out of the car. Her gravestone is easy to find. Farthest to the east on a plump little mound of hillside. She picked it out herself. I remember the morning. Rachel was already bald and starting to totter, her balance beginning to decline. I'd held her arm, like we were an ancient couple, picking out a site. But we weren't. We were barely cresting into our thirties, and I resented that fact so much that I couldn't even paste on a smile.

Today it's strangely easier. "Hey, babe," I say, sitting down on a patch of grass and looking at the headstone. "Man, I miss you." I put the flowers in the little vase to the side—the one the cemetery provides. "I met Gabby's birth mother. Crazy story, that one." Her headstone catches a ray of orange light. "And a lot of things happened. It made me realize I hadn't really dealt with some stuff. And..." I look around to be sure I'm alone. "I just wanted to say I'm sorry. I resented you dying. I resented you not telling me at the first inkling that you might be dying. I hated that you wanted to deal with that part alone. I felt like it was a secret from me, a piece all balled up and tucked away. Maybe it was, but you deserved to keep pieces, to move through it all in your own way. I told myself that, even then, but I didn't really believe it. All these years, I kind of resented it. Can you believe that? And I just wanted to say—" I choke a little on the words, glad the place is empty. "—that I don't anymore. I just loved you more than anything and that's exactly what made it all so hard. Ironic, huh? How loving someone can make it harder to let go, harder to forgive. How it can make the hurt hurt so much more. But I'm glad it hurt, glad that I could love you that much, glad that I wanted to glimpse every single piece of you, even if that was selfish. And if you were here, I hope that you'd love me enough to forgive me too, for my failings, my smallness."

A little late fall butterfly lights onto one of the daisies. Man, Rachel would have loved that. "Gabby's good," I say. "She likes her teacher, school." I hesitate. "She likes her birth mother too. And I was worried you might not be okay with that, um—on a few levels—but I actually think you really would, wouldn't you?" I can see the pollen on the butterfly's legs, actual pods from a thin lily that I hadn't noticed in the bouquet. It's a pale pink against the autumn golds. "I love you so much," I say, standing. "Always will."

The sun is warm; the air cool as I walk back to my car. It fits my mood. Shadow and sun, autumn and spring, life and death. We can't have one without the other, though it's easy to wish we could.

CHAPTER 41

*N*ora texts to say the baby I saved is out of the hospital.

"Great news!" I text back. I want to add something else, but don't know how to start. We both know what we know. Instead, I say, "How'd you find out?"

She calls. She can't seem to just text stuff. "Your chief called," she says. "He told me."

"Oh," I say, trying to sound nonchalant. *Is that all he told you?*

"He didn't call you?" she asks.

"Uh, not yet."

I think it kind of dawns on her then. "You gave him my number?"

"He saw you on the news. Asked about you. I'm really sorry if I overstepped. You're just a hot item."

"I'm not," she says bluntly. "I'm a big bruised apple."

I almost answer, *No, you're not.* But maybe she kind of is; maybe I kind of am too. "Nothing wrong with a few bruised apples."

"I'd rather be a shiny one."

"Would you? The bruised ones make the sweetest cider."

"It's more complicated than that, Aiden."

"I know," I say, "It's a lot complicated. And it's been a little confusing lately. *I've* been a little confused lately; and probably also confusing. Just basically all the versions of confused. Trying to sort some things out."

"Welcome to the club," she grumbles.

"Look," I say, "Maybe we should be confused together."

"I think we've already done that," she replies.

True enough. "Well, maybe we should try being not confused."

"That's a tall order for this situation."

"It is," I reply.

"And it won't be smooth. Even if we feel not confused, confusing things will just…come up."

They will. "But maybe we can try."

She doesn't answer.

"I feel ready to try," I reply.

273

"But why?" she finally says. "Why me? You could date a million women. I just don't think I'm probably the right one."

When she says it I realize that I really am done being confused, because I know that I could date other women, and I don't want to. "I'd like to try with you first," I say. And I feel it—that confidence that I haven't had.

"I don't know," she murmurs.

"Listen," I begin. "Let's just give a little trial. A testing period. We've only had one real date. Let's try a second. Two isn't too many. Especially when number one was so good."

"Number one wasn't the problem," she answers. "It was all the spaces in between."

"Those are the tricky parts in a relationship," I answer. "The spaces in between."

She kind of laughs at that, but I can tell she still isn't convinced.

"How about a little celebration. Because that baby's out of the hospital. Because we both worked together to save him."

"We did," she mutters. "We really did. And the kids are with their aunt," she adds. "That's the rumor anyway."

"Wow, you *are* in the know. And more good news." I pause. "*Do* you want to celebrate? With me."

She pauses on the other end of the line. "I don't know, Aiden."

"Of course, if you have plans..." I'm trying to be coy, but in reality I'm sweating, my hand slick on the phone.

"No," she interrupts. "No plans." Her voice gets a little sly. "Despite your best efforts, giving your chief my number."

"Please," I say. "I do owe you dessert. We never got our chocolate."

"You don't owe me anything," she says, echoing what I said weeks ago.

"Untrue," I add, my voice growing serious. "I owe you the biggest piece of light in my life."

"Aiden," she says, a warning in her voice.

"It's true," I add stubbornly, "and we might as well talk about it."

"It was a different life, a different me."

"And you did the right thing. You saved her life, mine. Maybe your own."

"Maybe," she whispers.

"So let's celebrate. We can talk more then."

She doesn't say anything. I'm not even sure she's still on the line.

"Please say yes," I add, surprised to hear the words. "Even if I don't deserve it."

She laughs, a sad-happy sound that I understand.

"Oh, Aiden," she says. "Everybody deserves dessert."

CHAPTER 42

PRESENT

Gabby's room is all pink. Rachel swore she'd never do the pink thing, so for those first few years, it remained a chipper yellow, but I always was the pushover parent. By the time the buck stopped at me, Gabby had distinct opinions, which all involved shades of pink. I cowed on the sheets first. She needed new ones and she picked out soft cotton with rainbows connecting to white clouds all on a backdrop of baby bottom pink. And what was a sheet? A gateway, that's what it was. Soon, the comforter to match was on clearance. After that, she complained about the 'baby poop' curtains—her words, not mine. They were replaced by bubblegum pink things with puffy valances. I didn't even know valances could be puffy. Truth be told, I didn't even know what valances were.

Pillowcases followed, a child-sized vanity for her hair things. All of it pink pink pink.

I'd put my foot down on the throw rug. It couldn't be the solid hot pink she wanted. Though we'd compromised on a flowered theme with pinks, blues, and yellows. Rachel would have liked the blue ones, I told myself. Though at this point, the battle was completely lost.

And there, at the center of the wall, the picture young Gabby had drawn of her and her mother, stick figures holding hands, Gabby wearing a bright pink triangle skirt, triangular bow in her hair. Surely Rachel had seen it coming, this pink, my weakness in the matter.

I touch the picture as I leave the room, imagine the waxy crayon under my fingers.

"Love you, Rachel."

CHAPTER 43

PRESENT

I tell Nora I'm taking her to my buddy's Shake Shoppe in Louisville. To her credit, she doesn't even bat an eye. I could have told her we were going to Denny's or the Ritz Carlton and I think she would have responded the exact same way.

"You long-time friends?" she asks, and it takes me a minute to remember my lie.

"High school," I say after the pause. "How's class going for you, by the way?"

"Straight A's right now," she says. "Which isn't saying much in community college, I guess, but if you'd told me I'd be getting *any* kind of A ten years ago, I would have laughed in your face."

"Just had to find yourself a little," I say.

"A lot," she adds. "Did you, uh…" She stops.

I glance at her.

"Did you tell your sister about me?"

"Yeah, she's watching Gabby."

"No," she says, "I mean, who I am in, uh, relation-ship to your family."

"Give her a few more weeks and she'll figure it out on her own. Kate's quick with stuff like that." The truth is that I had told her. Sort of. I'd told her about Nora's history with drugs, her sobriety, and that she'd once been a birth mother and given the baby up. I had a feeling that today Kate would stare into those green Gabby eyes and put two and two together. She really was good at that. How she would feel about it, well, I was less confident about that, but I knew that we could work it out. Kate was the type of person who moved forward, not back.

"Okay," Nora says, staring out the window at the trees flying by. "If you're sure."

"It's just a date," I say, giving her a quick poke in the side.

She squirms away from the tickle and I get my eyes back on the road. It's like we both know it's not just a date. We know it's *the* date, the one that will help us know how many should follow, if any. And I already have a feeling about it.

Just after we cross the bridge, I turn south and head toward a candy shop I read about. Over seventy varieties of chocolate. I pull into the parking lot and she cocks her head to the side, reading the sign.

"Not a shake," she says.

"Not yet," I smile, hopping out to get her door.

We wander the aisles for—no kidding—over an hour, selecting different pieces of chocolate. Along a display of darks her hand brushes mine as she leans forward to look at a truffle. I let my fingers dance for just a second along hers, twining two fingers through, then grasping her whole hand. She leans back, truffle forgotten, her eyes glistening, but uncertain. I don't let go.

We leave with several pounds of truffles and squares.

"Where should we eat them?" she asks, as we walk close together, our sides and hips brushing and bumping.

"Nowhere yet," I answer, grabbing her door and ushering her back into the car.

The next stop is the ice cream shop. "It's not all chocolate," I say, "but I had to improvise."

"I'll get the chocolatey-est chocolate one in the whole shop," she says. And she's not lying. She chooses the double devil chocolate in a chocolate-dipped waffle cone.

We eat them at a booth in the corner. Instead of

sitting across from her, I scoot in beside, my chocolate chocolate chip already starting to melt.

"Aiden," she says, when I'm tight against her. "Are you sure? It's so complicated."

I think about joking it away, saying, *It's just an ice cream booth.* But I don't. "It's a little complicated, yeah. But I can think of worse things."

"Like what?" she challenges.

"Like figuring out whether I should leave the job I love to be sure my little girl keeps her father."

Nora looks down at her ice cream and I wonder if I'm going in too far. "Or hearing that your wife has cancer. Or raising the perfect child." I smile.

She kind of does too. "Oh, that perfect child part can't be too hard," she says. "Easy peasy." She's still not looking at me though.

I take her chin, turn her to me. "And, correct me if I'm wrong, but I'm guessing that it's more complicated to leave an abusive boyfriend, give your baby up, find a job, start a new life."

"Oh, that's not the complicated part," she says, meeting my eyes. Hers swim with color, with depth. "The complicated part is leaving the old life behind, remembering every day that the person before isn't the now me, isn't the now life, that it never will be again. Do you think that's a thing we would both be able to do?"

The ice cream is dripping across my fingers and I feel for a small moment like Gabby. "Truth is, I think we already did the complicated part, at least I did. I decided something. And here I am."

Her face tips forward, mouth only an inch from mine, silky red hair falling over her shoulder. "Cheers, then," she says, her voice husky and low. When she suddenly leans over, and steals a bite of my ice cream. Quick as a wink.

"Hey!" I say, trying to get a bite of hers, which she masterfully maneuvers away from me. "You tricked me."

"It was easy," she says, still holding her cone up high as I reach over and try to get it. I put a hand around her waist, and she laughs, that wind chime of a sound. And then I see the kid at the counter staring at us, and we both giggle, remembering that we're two adults in an ice cream shop.

"You ready for the next stop?" I whisper.

"There's another one?" she asks.

"Well, it wouldn't be much of a chocolate bar re-creation without at least one more."

Her eyes, they sort of melt then. "Oh, Aiden, it's probably the nicest thing anyone has done for me. Well, not counting Joe and Brenda giving me that job."

"Well, it's not over," I say, taking her hand and

helping her out of the booth, right before I lean over and take a swift bite of her ice cream. The rest almost falls on the floor and she gasps. "You turd!"

"Ha!" I say. "Got you back."

The next spot, second to last, is a bakery called the "Chocohaul." It's fitting.

"Oh my," she says when we walk through the door. "It's like diabetes in a box. I'm going to need another twelve-step program." For a second, she freezes up, worrying that she's over-stepped, but then I laugh. And then she does. We get two choco-late donuts, one huge mint chocolate brownie, an assortment of mini cookies no bigger than quarters, and a perfectly symmetrical cube of chocolate éclair.

Her skin glows as we leave, her cheeks a deep flush from laughing. I slip an arm around her waist, whisper. "And one more stop to eat it all."

"I am *not* eating it all," she whispers back, letting her forehead tip against mine. So delicious, that face.

"Well, a start then."

She begins to walk to the car, but I tug her back. I'm only a couple inches taller than she is, though probably twice as broad at the shoulders. The soft-ness of her would fold perfectly against my chest. I breathe in, imagining it, the heat of her body, her fire soft cheeks. I pull her a little closer.

"We going?" she says, tipping away just as I'm ready to lean in. But she's not fooling me. Her cheeks are deep pink, down to her neck.

I reach out and run my fingers along her hot skin.

"Gonna need all kinds of twelve-step programs by the time the night is done," she murmurs, and I take her hand, our arms swinging between us, as we walk to my car.

It's dusk by the time we arrive at the park tucked away in the outskirts of Louisville, but the gates are still open. "I brought a blanket," I say.

She doesn't answer, just steps out of the car, admiring the lights of the city in the distance. "You know I'm from the deep country, right?"

"I know your accent gives it away occasionally."

"I still haven't driven in a city bigger than Haydensboro."

"Well, maybe we can remedy that tonight."

"No," she says. "Not tonight."

"Another night then," I say.

"Yeah, another."

I take the thermos from my trunk, along with two thick mugs and a woolly blanket.

"Last stop?" she asks.

"Yup," I say.

"How'd you find this place?"

"Google maps," I answer. "It was either this or Lover's Peak."

"Oh dear," she says. "Those were the only two choices, huh?"

"I think I chose right," I say. "What do you think?"

"For tonight," she says. "For tonight."

I pour hot chocolate from the thermos into her mug, add a dash of vanilla syrup and hand it to her. It already feels like the autumn dew is settling from the air onto our shoulders, and the steam from the cocoa billows through the cool, humid air.

"This was nice, Aiden," she says as I open up the box of baked goods and scoot them close to her.

She looks at the box. "I don't even think I can choose."

"Then don't," I say, "You can have a little bit of everything." I break off a piece of donut and, without thinking, pop it into her mouth. Her lips brush my fingers, and I hold my hand against her face. She leans in to my palm, her cheek hot. I lean in to her— pulling her forehead to mine. Noses touch, lips warm.

We hold there for a velvet moment, breathing. And then I press my lips to hers, hot like flames. Her mouth, cheeks, burning into me.

When she breaks away, I still hold her face close, look into her eyes. Not worlds like Gabby's were to me, but oceans, swimming and deep.

"Now your turn." She chooses the éclair, breaks a corner off the messy dessert. "You're better at this than I am."

"It's perfect," I say, and she pops it into her own mouth instead of mine.

"Hey!" I say.

On and on like that—sharing cookies and truffles and bon bons.

"We better go home," she whispers. "Before we wind up on Lover's Peak."

"I can think of worse fates," I say, as I help her to her feet, then pull her in again. Her hair falls over my neck and she does fold into me, sweet and soft, though I can feel the tight, long muscles, the fight and struggle that got her to where she is now. "But I gotta tuck Gabby in."

"She's a lucky girl," Nora says. "The luckiest."

I push Nora's hair over her shoulder, let my hand cup against her neck. "I think she is lucky. And me too."

EPILOGUE

$\mathcal{N}$atalie's got carpool today, and I stand in Gabby's room, pretending I've just wandered in, but knowing I came here for a reason. The picture she drew hangs over her dresser, mounted in my grief five years ago. A stick mother holding the stick fingers of her little girl. This mother has curly brown hair. She's missing a lot of the curves I remember, which is to be expected from a stick lady, but she is wearing a red dress—my favorite color on her. Gabby made her own hair blond, but drew it wavy to match her mother's. Her *mother's*.

"She'll always be yours," I tell the drawing. It stares straight ahead, still smiling. "I will too," I continue. "We're just both making room for something new. Is that okay with you?"

I close my eyes and the picture transforms in my mind. The day Gabby came home with us, bundled into that brand new car seat. Both of us "parents"— and it felt like it needed some air quotes—the way we fumbled around with it. Buckles and blankets. Gabby wailing from the back of the car. Rachel cracking her knuckles, blowing out a gust of frustrated breath.

"Second thoughts?" I'd asked, only half joking.

"Never," she'd said, that ready smile. "Never never."

I'd leaned over the front seat, kissed her at the stoplight, like a couple of teenagers.

Gabby had stayed up all that night. And the next. So many nights of pacing with a screaming baby. We'd frayed, thinned, but I'd held onto it, that kiss, Rachel's smile. She held on too—to whatever it was that had kept her going—and soon enough we fell in love with that screeching bald bundle of baby; and that baby fell in love with us. What more could we ask for? I wouldn't have complained about forty more years, but the universe wasn't taking requests. "She'll always be yours," I repeat. "But is it okay, this other person? Is it really okay?"

In that moment, I hear her cooing voice, caramel smooth, see her round dark lips, full and tender. And her teeth—white, clean, with that one so perfectly crooked. Just like our lives had been.

"Of course," she says. "There's always room for something new, something good."

ACKNOWLEDGMENTS

Many wonderful people contribute to the writing of a book. It's nice to get a chance to thank them. First of all, a huge thank you to all the unsung heroes in our communities—both the amazing EMS workers and the foster/adoptive parents. You all make our world a better place.

Specifically, I'd like to thank Kip and John for their insights into EMS and firefighting, and Sadie for giving me information on how the foster and adoption process works. I also couldn't have written this without a little insight from my once-addict-now-clean-for-twenty-five-years friend, Laura.

Additionally, I'd love to thank my wonderful beta readers, Michelle and Naomi. They gave me excellent insight about what was working and what wasn't. When all those changes were done, my final editor, Carrie, came in and cleaned up any remaining messes. Thank you.

Finally, I want to thank my husband, Kip, and my kids for all the support they give me during a writing project. Writing takes time, and time is finite. Thanks for allowing (because we all know they could make it heck if they wanted to...) me to take pieces of it for myself and this book.

.

READ MORE!

If you enjoyed this book, subscribe to my newsletter! You'll get the prequel story, "Ready," for free, as well as updates on upcoming novels, sales, and local events. You can subscribe from my website, jeanknightpace.com.

Looking for some stories about real life heroes? Check out *Pulse: A Paramedic's Walk Along the Lines of Life and Death*.

It's a collection of essays by my very own husband (his stories, written by me) along with a few of my own essays, which tell the spouses side of the story.

And finally, if you're **interested in reading the true life story of an addict and her recovery,** you can check out the memoir, *Four Seconds*. Read about it below.

In her debut memoir, Laura Andrade tells of her years with cocaine and crystal methamphetamines—using, then selling—until all she had left of the life she wanted was a chalk outline and a pack of cigarettes. This is the story of her use and recovery, of the people who frustrated and inspired her, of her decision to leave the drug world. It is the story of her slow, often unsteady walk home.

Laura told me her story; I helped her find the words for it.

ABOUT THE AUTHOR

J.E. Pace (who also writes under the name Jean Knight Pace) is the co-author of the YA novels, *Grey Stone* and *Grey Lore.* Her other works include *Hugging Death: Essays on Motherhood and Saying Goodbye* as well as *Four Seconds.* She lives in Indiana with her husband, four children, eight ducks, four chickens, and a cat. You can find more about her at jeanknightpace.com

Made in the USA
Columbia, SC
22 September 2023

23209875R00178